BLACK DIAMOND

VICTORIA QUINN

ROME

Living with Christopher wasn't quite as strange as I expected.

The apartment was big enough that we didn't need to share much space. He had the master bedroom with his own bathroom and shower. I used the guest bathroom near the living room, so we didn't get in each other's way in the morning before work. Neither one of us ate much, so sharing food wasn't a problem either. We went to the grocery store once a week and purchased the bare essentials, but dirty dishes never piled up in the sink because neither one of us used them.

Of course, Christopher brought women back to the apartment often. When they first looked at me, they despised me, viewing me as a threat. But once

Christopher explained I was his poor sister who needed to shack up with him, they actually cracked a smile.

But other than that, everything was fine.

I didn't need a driver to take me to work because my office was just two blocks away. Calloway didn't mind my walking there, especially since Christopher had to head that direction anyway. So I had someone to keep me company on the short journey.

I came home after work one afternoon to find Christopher on the couch, placing a cold beer on a coaster. He was still in his collared shirt and tie, his jacket hanging over the back of the couch. "Hey."

"Yo." He didn't take his eyes off the TV. "How are the stinky homeless people?"

I set my purse on the counter and pulled out my phone. "Christopher, don't call them that."

"What?" he asked. "It's not like it's untrue."

"But even so."

"We were stinky homeless people once upon a time." He continued to stare at the screen even though he didn't seem truly interested in it.

I dropped the conversation because it was pointless anyway. "How was work?"

"Good. Stocks are high. I'm doing a lot of selling."

I'd never cared for his profession or tried to

understand it. It was far too mathematical and unpredictable for me to truly care about. I'd always been interested in the behaviors of people and society, not making money.

I grabbed the mail sitting on the counter and rifled through it, not seeing anything for me. I'd changed my mailing address to this apartment so I didn't have to head to my post office box all the time. If Hank really wanted to bother me, he could come here. My bat would love to say hello.

I slipped off my heels and fell into the armchair, my feet finally relaxing after a long day of walking around my office.

"How's Prince Charming?"

"I don't know who you're referring to." I eyed the TV, seeing a cartoon. Christopher was a grown man who was successful and intelligent, but he still acted like a child. Since neither one of us had really had a childhood, I didn't give him shit for it.

"Oh, come on. Yes, you do."

"You mean my sexy boyfriend?"

He rolled his eyes. "Sure. Whatever."

"Good. He's glad I moved in here with you."

"I bet," he said with a chuckle. "That way I can make sure you don't do anything stupid."

"I never do stupid things," I countered.

"You fought a thug who broke into your apartment, busted your lip, and bruised your face." He turned his eyes to me, giving me a glare. "Yes, you do stupid stuff."

Calloway and Christopher would throw that in my face forever. "Okay, that's the one stupid thing that I've done."

"Ro, I have a list. But I don't have the energy to go through the whole thing. So, are you going to his place for dinner?"

I picked up on his train of thought. "Trying to get rid of me because you have a hot date coming over?"

"I wouldn't call her a hot date. Just a fuck buddy that's in town for a business meeting."

Christopher usually gave me a heads-up when he needed to be alone in the apartment, and I appreciated the notification so I could find something else to do. I definitely didn't want to be here for their hump-a-thon. "I'll go to Calloway's place."

"Perfect."

As if he knew we were talking about him, Calloway called.

"Ooh," Christopher said. "It's Prince Charming…"

I ignored the nickname and took the call. "Hey, sexy."

Christopher cringed then walked into his bedroom

on the other side of the apartment, not wanting to listen to this conversation.

Deep and powerful, Calloway's masculine voice came through the phone. "Hey, Vanilla."

I'd become used to the nickname even though I didn't really feel vanilla anymore. "Are you free tonight? I need to get out of the apartment because Christopher is having company—the slutty kind."

"You know you're always welcome here."

"So, that's a yes?"

"A big yes." Whenever he spoke to me, he always had very little to say, and he always got to the point. He seemed to issue commands more often than participate in a fluid conversation. "So, get over here."

I stopped by the store and picked up a few things before I knocked on his front door.

To my delight, he was only in his sweatpants, his chiseled chest looking far more appetizing than the food I just bought. He looked me up and down with the same desire, his eyes black as coal. "Sweetheart." His powerful arm, corded with veins, wrapped around my waist, and he pulled me inside.

I dropped the bag onto the hardwood floor and

wrapped my arms around his tight waist. His skin was searing hot in comparison to the cold weather outside. My nails automatically dug into him just the way they did when we made love. My claws sank into him because I never wanted to let go.

He kissed my neck and moved his lips along my jawline until he kissed my chin. Slowly, he moved to my lips before he gave me a scorching kiss right on the mouth. He breathed into me, his arms constricting me like a snake suffocating its prey. He devoured me like he'd been thinking about me all day, waiting for this moment when we were reunited. "Missed you, Vanilla."

"I always miss you." Whenever he kissed me, I lost my resolve. I turned into a weak woman, my knees unable to keep my frame straight. He did incredible things to me, making me lose all logic and focus. A part of me loved the effect he had on me—but another part hated it. My heart was losing the battle for power, and slowly, I was surrendering to this ruthless warlord. I didn't mind living with Christopher, but I would give anything to live with Calloway again. After only knowing each other for a few months, it immediately felt right.

"Good." He pressed his lips to my ear. "That must mean I'm doing something right."

I wrapped my arms around his neck and pressed my

face against his chest, feeling so safe with this strong man. My backbone was rigid with pride. I never let my walls down, but they were slowly crumbling. And the worst part was, I wanted them to crumble. I trusted this man as much as I trusted my own brother. The world didn't seem so cold and unforgiving when I had Calloway in my life.

He rested his chin on my head as he held me in the doorway, his hard chest expanding with every breath he took. "Everything alright, sweetheart?"

Everything was perfect—and that was the problem. I was falling hard, and I actually enjoyed it. "Everything is great. I just like it when you hold me like this."

He moved his lips to my forehead and pressed a gentle kiss against my skin. "Then I'll hold you like this forever."

After minutes of savoring the touch, I pulled away. "I brought dinner. I thought I could make some salmon, veggies, and rice."

"That sounds amazing." He looked at me with those beautiful blue eyes and handsome features. He had a strong jaw, a perfect nose, and a chin that made him look kingly. When he stared at me like I was his queen, I felt like royalty.

"Then I'll get to work." I walked into the kitchen and set everything on the counter.

Calloway leaned against the kitchen island, watching me with interest. He crossed his arms over his massive chest as he watched me wash the vegetables and dice them on the cutting board. He didn't make a comment about anything I was doing, content just to watch me.

"What?" I asked, keeping my eyes on my handiwork.

"I like to watch you. You fascinate me."

I chuckled. "Because I'm cooking for you." After I finished preparing everything, I shoved the pan in the oven and turned on the timer.

"Because of so much more, actually." He crowded me against the counter, using his large size to press me against the wood. Once he had me cornered, he pressed his hips into me, his cock hard through his pants. He moved his lips down my neck, gently kissing and teasing me.

I closed my eyes and enjoyed it, loving it when he pinned me like this. I was his to enjoy, and I loved being devoured like wild prey.

Slowly, he began to undress me, removing my dress, bra, and panties. When I stood naked in his kitchen, he pulled his sweatpants off, over six feet of pure man. His long cock was pressed between us, warm against my stomach.

He kissed the corner of my mouth before he walked away into his living room. He sat back in the center of the couch, his back against the cushion. His thick dick lay against his stomach, seeping pre-come as he waited for me to join him.

I stood in front of him, my naked body on display for him to study.

He grabbed the base of his cock and gently massaged it as he looked at me. It was the hottest scene I'd ever witnessed. He locked his eyes with mine, not the least bit self-conscious about me watching him. "Ride me. Now." He turned authoritative, speaking to me like a commanding officer.

I didn't appreciate the bossiness when we were spending time together, but the moment things turned sexual between us, I couldn't get enough of it. I liked not thinking. I liked not having to make decisions. I liked letting go, trusting someone else to guide me.

I crawled into his lap and straddled his hips, feeling the head of his cock against my entrance. I'd never taken him this way, and my stomach clenched nervously. He wasn't just long, but impressively thick. It was a new angle, one I'd never tried before. My experience paled in comparison to his, but he never seemed to mind.

Calloway took the lead, like always. "Play with your tits." His expression was ice-cold, suggesting defiance wasn't an option.

I palmed both of my breasts and massaged them.

Calloway grabbed my hips and slowly pulled me onto his length, pushing through my tightness as he slid into me. Inch by inch, he entered my slick channel.

My hands stopped moving, and I winced and moaned nearly at the same time, absorbing the pleasure and disregarding the pain. We'd been sleeping together for nearly a month, but the pain of intercourse was prevalent. Our anatomical differences must have been the cause, but I wouldn't want it to change anything even if I had the power to make it happen. Because the discomfort was nothing in comparison to how good he made me feel. His cock made me feel so full, like a sexy woman.

He pulled me into his lap, every inch of his length buried inside me.

My hands left my tits and wrapped around his strong wrists, gripping the corded veins across his hands and forearms. My pussy stretched the longer he sat inside me, my narrow channel acclimating slowly.

"Play with your tits." His face was inches from mine

as he issued the same command as he had before. He didn't move until I obeyed.

My hands returned to the sensitive skin, feeling my hard nipples brush against my fingertips.

He watched me with a dark expression, loving the sight. His jaw clenched, and a moan so quiet I barely heard it escaped his lips. His hands moved underneath my thighs, and he guided me up and down his length, his hips rocking into me slowly. "Pinch your nipples."

I'd never heard of someone pinching their own nipples, so I didn't do it. I massaged my breasts slowly, feeling the smooth skin and the round shape.

"Twist. Your. Nipples." He pulled me down his length again, impaling me with this size.

A haze had fallen over me, and I couldn't see straight anymore. All I could see was this gorgeous man, the king of sex, commanding me to do something. His hard cock was deep inside me, so he had the power to rule my body.

I did as he asked, twisting them mildly until I felt a spike of pain. I moaned quietly through the pain until I felt the influx of pleasure. It floored me because I didn't expect it. Not once did I consider touching myself like that when I was alone with my vibrator.

He moved me up and down again, the lust deep in his eyes. "Rock your hips. Like this." He gripped my ass and then made the motion for me, teaching me how to arch my back before I slid down his length. Each time I did it, my clit rubbed against his pelvic bone in just the right away—and it felt amazing.

"Oh god…" My hands left my breasts, and I touched his chest, feeling the powerful muscle and grooves of his abs. I slid my hands to his shoulders and used them as an anchor so I could dig my hips deeper. We were still moving together at a slow pace, but the speed didn't hinder the pleasure—it only heightened it.

"Jesus fucking Christ, you look sexy." His hands moved up my stomach to my tits, where he palmed each one. He squeezed my nipples between his thumbs and forefingers and gave them a gentle pinch.

I winced but moaned again, inexplicably addicted to the sensation. The moisture from my pussy dripped down his length all the way to his balls. I could feel the slickness every time I ground against his hips, knowing I was overflowing with arousal.

My hips moved quicker, grinding against him and taking in his length. I rubbed my nub against his hard skin, feeling my orgasm approaching in the distance. There was a fire deep in my belly, a power surging through my veins. My nails dug into his shoulders, and I locked my eyes with his, crumbling before I even hit my threshold.

"I knew I had to have you the second I laid eyes on you..." He guided my hips harder, making me move faster up and down his length. "Beautiful. Strong. And you've got one hell of an arm on you."

I don't know what possessed me to do it, but I slapped him hard across the face—hard enough to leave a mark. His face turned with the hit, and he closed his eyes as he released a quiet moan. His hips didn't stop thrusting, and his cock twitched noticeably deep inside me.

He slowly turned back to me, his eyes burning like the center of the sun. "Fuck, baby." He clenched his jaw, his arousal increasing as his skin continued to redden in response to my palm. His hand moved between my legs, and he rubbed me aggressively, circling my clit with a perfect motion. "Come, sweetheart. Because I know I'm about to."

My nails dug into his shoulders as I felt the explosion between my legs. I tightened around him, squeezing him as the rush surged through me. "Calloway..." I loved saying his name. It rolled off my tongue with possessiveness, loving the fact that this man was mine to treasure. "Oh god..."

He shoved himself deep inside me as he released, reaching his threshold while I finished off the rest of mine. His heavy come filled me, the weight significant and warm. He pressed his lips to mine as he finished, his breathing deep and heavy.

After the moment had passed, he kept me on top of him. He leaned back against the couch and gripped my thighs, his cock softening inside me. He watched me with his lidded eyes, his expression dark with obsession.

The timer went off on the oven, announcing the food had finished cooking. Just when I moved to get off him, he pulled me back onto his length, refusing to pull out of me. "Forget the food. You're staying right here." He pulled me against his chest and kissed the corner of my mouth, waiting to get hard so he could fuck me again.

I almost obeyed, wanting to stay connected to this glorious man. But my beliefs were too strong to be ignored. "I can't waste food." The impulse was deep in my gut. I wouldn't even throw away a half-eaten container of yogurt. When I made a big meal, I ate it every single day until it was completely gone.

Calloway wanted to fight me. It was obvious in the expression he gave me. But he yielded his power and released me, understanding this was important to me. He relinquished his need to control the situation and let me go. Once his hands were off me, they curled into fists, the silent sign of his frustration.

"Thank you." I left his lap, his wet dick thudding

against his stomach once I was back on my feet. I could still feel the weight of his come inside me, knowing it was slowly sliding down to my entrance. He intended to add another load after dinner.

And I looked forward to it.

2

CALLOWAY

I loved the way she twisted her nipples. Self-conscious at first, she was reluctant. But when she saw how hot she made me, she gave it a try. She twisted her nipples fearlessly, causing enough pain to make her wince but enough pleasure to make her moan. The sensitive skin around her nipples reddened, and the sight aroused me further.

Her virginity was initially a disappointment, but now I enjoyed teaching her new positions. When she straddled my hips, I could tell it was something she'd never done before. But she listened to my instruction and allowed me to guide her, to teach her how to sheathe my cock over and over again. I showed her how to grind her clit against my pelvic bone, a new realm of pleasure for her. She was a quick learner, and by the end, she was a pro.

Once I knew she was open to the idea, I pinched her nipples.

I didn't do it as harshly as I wanted, but I still tested the waters to see her reaction. Thankfully, she liked it, biting her lip in a sexy way that turned me on like nothing else. She had the innocence of a virgin but the courage of a warrior.

That gave me hope.

She looked at me differently from the way she used to, offering me a new level of trust she'd never shown before. She was at ease around me, unafraid to express her true opinions. But the best part of all was her vulnerability.

There wasn't a single wall inside her heart.

I had her exactly where I wanted her.

After a few months of getting to know one another, I would finally tell her what I wanted. And I had faith that our mutual feelings would be enough for us to achieve that new level. She wouldn't let anyone else tie her to a headboard or spank her ass until it was red — but she would make an exception for me.

After dinner, we went into my bedroom on the top floor and dropped our clothes once more. I wanted to keep going earlier, but her devotion to not wasting food interrupted the heat of the moment. If she were anyone else, I would have commanded her to remain on my dick and not allowed her to leave until I gave her explicit permission.

But Rome was different.

I got her on her back in my bed, her tits firm and perky. Instead of sliding into home plate, I lay on top of her and cherished her with endless kisses. I tasted every inch of her skin, enjoying the hint of vanilla from her lotion. When her nipples were in my mouth, they pebbled into a point, and I sucked them harshly until she winced. I wanted her nipples to ache for the rest of the night and the following morning—so she wouldn't forget about me. My mouth moved to her ear next, breathing deeply into her canal. "On your knees."

She dragged her nails down my back, comfortable underneath me with her ankles hooked around my waist. I liked her there too, but I wanted her ass in the air. I wanted to stare at that gorgeous asshole while I fucked her from behind.

When she didn't move, I breathed into her ear again. "Now."

She cupped my face and gave me a slow kiss, one full of tongue and desire. She breathed gently into my mouth, her moans audible from the inside out. The kiss was so sexy I forgot about the command I gave her altogether.

She turned over and separated her knees, looking at

me over her shoulder with her lips parted. Those green eyes sparkled in the dim lighting of my bedroom, silently begging for my cock to enter her.

I'd never been with a woman who wanted me more.

The fact that she wanted me because of me, not my wealth or looks, just made it better.

I leaned back on the balls of my feet and slipped into her, my head pushing through her tight channel and inching deep inside. She was soaked for me — constantly. I pushed until I was balls deep, stretching her deliciously.

I grabbed her by the back of the neck, my fingers squeezing her hard. I took a deep breath and forced my fingers to relax, knowing I couldn't be so firm with her yet. I pressed her head to the mattress, her ass sticking up farther in the air.

I planted one foot on the bed then gripped her hips as I thrust into her, fucking her hard. I took her gently earlier because that was the particular mood I was in. But now, my dominance was in control, and I wanted to take her roughly and make her scream.

My hand ached to slap her ass.

In fact, it burned.

I rubbed her cheek as I thrust into her, loving the petite muscles of her back and shoulders. She was slender but defined with strength. Her hair was sprawled out on the sheets with her face pressed to the mattress, her moans sometimes muffled against the bed.

My hand shook as it caressed her cheek. When my control slipped away, I slapped my palm against her ass —mildly. It wasn't nearly as hard as I wanted to strike her. It was just a test, to see her reaction over something minor.

She moaned a little louder, her reaction to the touch not exactly clear.

I leaned over her, my chest pressed against her back. The sweat from my body rubbed against hers, our hot and writhing bodies working together to heighten the sex. She turned her head over her shoulder, her mouth open and begging for a kiss.

I crushed my mouth against hers and shoved my tongue into her throat, swallowing her moans. My cock buried itself inside her with every thrust, wanting to go deeper. She was always so wet for me, making it possible for me to push so far inside her. I had worried her little pussy would never take my fat cock with ease.

I grabbed her wrists and held them behind her back, owning her more intimately. An image of rope appeared in my mind, and I imagined it tied around her petite wrists, the painful friction rubbing harshly into her skin. I imagined her as my prisoner, with no escape unless I permitted it. It didn't matter if she had somewhere to be. She would only walk away when I gave her permission.

The thoughts made me so goddamn hard.

I squeezed her wrists tighter then spanked her again, this time, a little harder.

"Calloway..." She let out a scream as she came, exploding on impact. Her back arched as she absorbed the pleasure, the mattress muffling her screams as she writhed underneath me. The orgasm seemed to stretch on forever because it was a full minute before her screams died away.

Now I wanted to release. I gripped her wrists tighter and gave her a few more pumps, finding my threshold almost instantly. I shoved my cock all the way inside her, nearly hitting her cervix as I came with a moan. "Vanilla..." I leaned over her and pressed my lips against the center of her spine, feeling my cock release my load into her channel. Every time I filled her, I felt like a king.

And she was my queen.

When I walked into my office at Ruin, Jackson was already there.

He was sitting in the high-back chair and facing my

desk, his blue eyes following me as I walked around and sat in the chair on the opposite side. His fingers brushed against the scruff of his chin, appearing indifferent even though he obviously felt the opposite. "Numbers are the same. We should be growing. That's what businesses do."

"We don't have the room." I didn't need to look at the numbers to understand what Jackson was talking about. "If we have too many members, everything will be crowded, and people will stop showing."

"And yet, gyms do it all the time. Never enough cardio machines, and the weight room is always packed."

I was used to his sarcasm, so it no longer affected me. "No."

"Then we should open that second location that we talked about."

"No." With two businesses, I was already tied down. Now that I had Rome around every day, my time was even more restricted. It was difficult for me to come to Ruin without Rome figuring out what I was really doing.

"Is that the only word you know how to say?" He straightened in his chair, giving me a hateful look.

"To you, yes."

He rolled his eyes, clearly pissed off. "Then what do we do?"

"We enjoy the success and live our lives."

"Dad always said if a business isn't growing, it's failing."

Like I didn't remember. Our father drilled his experience into me every single day. Like a messiah, he pretended to know all the answers. "We're fine, Jackson. It'll only make Ruin more exclusive, and we can raise the prices for members. We can double the revenue without doubling the members. That's better, if you ask me."

If Jackson had a comeback, he would have said something by now. But he remained silent in his chair, staring me down with even more rage. He hated me for being wrong, but he absolutely loathed me for being right. Tired of living in my shadow, he let his anger make him do even more immature things.

"So, we're sticking with our original plan. Things could be worse, Jackson. So, lighten up."

"I'll lighten up when Rome is out of the picture."

I knew he would bring her up. It was only a matter of time. "What's your problem, Jackson?" He never stuck his nose into my love life, but now he was obsessed with it. I never showed curiosity about the women he dated. I couldn't care less where he put his dick.

"I told you my problem in the bar weeks ago." He stared me down with his typical threatening edge.

"She's not changing me."

"Fine. Keep lying to yourself."

"Not that it's any of your business, but she and I are making progress. When she's ready, I'll tell her the truth. I'll introduce her to the underworld and turn her into the devil himself. I'll be at your beck and call all over again. So, just chill."

"Seriously?" He cocked his head to the side, examining me closely.

"Yes. Seriously."

"What does that mean? She's into kinky shit?"

She liked it when I twisted her nipples and spanked her ass. She was definitely open to new things besides vanilla sex. When we were in the heat of the moment, she would obey my commands. I wished she would do it all the time, but I'd settle for that. "Something like that."

"What about Isabella?"

"What about her?" I hadn't been with her in three months, yet she always came up. Honestly, I didn't even think about her.

"She still wants you."

So desperate. So weak. So undesirable. "That's her

problem, not mine. So what's new with you, Jackson? Who are you humping?"

He ignored the comment.

"Sorry, am I being too nosy?" I asked sarcastically.

"Fuck you, Cal." He finally walked out of my office, slamming the door behind him. For just a moment, the sound of techno dance music entered my office. The bass thudded against the walls, mimicking the migraine beginning behind my eyes.

"Fuck you too."

3

ROME

I t was noon.

Christopher was coming by my office to pick me up for lunch. Even though we lived together, we didn't see each other as often as I thought we would. So when he asked me to get sandwiches for lunch, I agreed.

The bell rang overhead, and I immediately stood up and grabbed my purse. I had a short lunch break because I had a meeting with a donor at one. We were organizing a canned food drive all over the city. Several department stores had agreed to participate. "I'm in a hurry today, so let's save the chitchat and get going—" My mouth shut when I came face-to-face with Hank.

Great.

He was handsome in his suit and tie, but the look was deceptive. He came in a pretty package, but he was an evil monster on the inside. As the DA of New York City, he had more power than any single man should have. And he used it to his advantage—in the cruelest ways. "Hey, honey. You look nice today."

I grabbed my purse and reached for the bat I kept under the table.

"Oh, no. Not that again." He moved his massive body in my way, leaning against the desk and crossing his arms over his chest.

"I don't need a bat to kick your ass." I kept my arms by my sides and tried to think of other things to grab. Thankfully, Calloway had sent me a large vase of flowers that would be perfect to smash over his head. "I can do that just fine on my own."

He grinned, but it was utterly disturbing. "I've always liked that fire in you. Sexy—"

When his eyes were locked on mine, I kicked him between the legs.

He turned his knee and blocked it, slightly wincing from the tip of my heel. "Nice try, sweetheart. You'll have to step it up."

"Get out of my office."

"No." He crossed his arms over his chest. "I'm inviting you to dinner tonight. There's something I want to talk about."

"You can have dinner with my answering machine."

I snatched my purse and headed for the door. I didn't care enough about my office to defend it from a sick motherfucker like him.

"Oh, I don't think so—"

The bell rang overhead, and Christopher walked inside. "You ready for lunch? Dude, I'm starving—" The words died in his mouth when he spotted Hank behind me, just about to grab me before I got through the door. Still shocked, Christopher stood there as he took a moment to absorb what he was looking at.

I knew he was about to snap.

"You wanna die, you piece of shit?" Christopher charged him, using his size and strength to barrel Hank down.

But I got in the way. "Christopher, no." I pushed him back then grabbed him by the arm. "He's not worth it. You know the second you touch him, he'll sue your ass and get your license taken away."

Christopher pushed me back. "Couldn't care less." He darted for Hank again.

I grabbed Christopher by the shoulders and pushed him toward the door. "No. He's not worth it for you or me." I managed to get him through the door and to the sidewalk. "Now, let's walk away."

"No. Let's call the cops."

We could've done that, but no good would've come of it. "We know that's not gonna get us anywhere."

"So we do nothing?" he asked incredulously. "Is this not the first time he's shown up at your work like this?"

I pressed my lips together tightly.

Christopher blew up all over again. "Rome, this is unacceptable." He kept eyeing the door, waiting for Hank to come out so he could rip his throat out.

"We've been down this road many times. Nothing we do works against him. He's too powerful. All we can do is go about our lives and not let him drag us down. So, let's go eat."

Christopher twisted out of my grasp and walked away, too pissed off to even look at me. He walked up to the stop sign and punched the pole so hard he left a dent in the metal. Everyone nearby stopped and stared, looking at him like he was a loose cannon. Christopher eyed them. "What the fuck are you looking at?"

Christopher ordered a sandwich, but for the first time, he didn't eat his food. He leaned back into the booth and stared out the window, his mouth in a permanent grimace. Bloodlust was in his eyes, his hands desperate to strangle Hank until he stopped breathing.

I picked at my food, not very hungry either. I wished Christopher hadn't witnessed the ordeal at my office. He was playful and humorous all the time, but he had a serious temper problem that derived from his childhood. When he was worked up, he made a lot of stupid decisions—like hitting people. While I thought Hank deserved an ass-kicking, he could do some serious damage to Christopher if he felt like it. Being close to the police department, the judges, and other lawyers allowed Hank to monopolize the entire justice system.

"Christopher…" I reached across the table and rested my hand on his.

Christopher yanked it away. "Don't fucking touch me right now." He kept his voice low so no one else would hear us. "Does Calloway know about this?" He finally looked at me, the hatred in his eyes obvious.

God, no.

Absolutely not.

I could only imagine what would happen if he did.

"No," I finally answered. "And he's not gonna know, so keep your mouth shut."

"Fuck no. Calloway is rich, and he knows people. Of course I'm telling him."

That was something I couldn't let happen.

"Christopher, this is my business and not his. Do not tell him."

"Watch me."

"I'm serious."

"And you think I'm joking?" he snapped. "He needs to know you have a psychotic ex following you around."

"Hank left me alone for a long time. I'm not sure why he's made a resurgence."

"And you better not find out," he said through gritted teeth. "Thank fucking god you're living with me. I'm not letting you move out unless it's with Calloway."

The thing I loved most about Christopher was his innate calmness. He was always carefree and easygoing. He was never overprotective of me, especially after we became adults. He encouraged me to go out and live my life. But the second I was threatened, disrespected, or in danger, he flipped out. "Please don't tell him, Christopher. It's important to me."

"Why would you not tell him? He's your boyfriend, right?"

"Yes." He was more than just my boyfriend. My heart was twisted so hard around his fingers that I could never get free. "But Calloway is..." He was difficult to put into words. "I really think he might kill Hank."

Christopher smiled, but it was in a ruthless,

terrifying kind of way. "Good. Then I should definitely tell him."

"I don't want Calloway to ruin his reputation and his company over this. I really believe Hank will leave me alone. I'm not afraid of him. If he lays a hand on me, trust me, I'll kick his ass."

"But not before he breaks your arm again."

Sorrow washed over me with the memory. Christopher had sat beside me at the hospital, so angry he cried. I didn't want to relive that moment, to see Christopher feeling so bad for me that he felt bad too. "Everything will be okay. There's no need to get so worked up."

He shook his head.

"We need to keep this between us."

"I think you're being really unfair to Calloway. He should know what he's dealing with. It's wrong to keep him in the dark like this."

"I'll tell him." My feelings for Calloway were undeniably clear. The second I gave myself to him, I knew how I felt. He was the man I'd been waiting all my life to meet. He was the male version of myself. I wanted to share everything about my soul with him — but not all at once. "I just don't want to drop this on him right now. We're still getting to know one another."

"You've been dating for three months," Christopher

hissed. "You should know everything about each other by now."

"Not us. We're taking it slow."

He rolled his eyes. "I'll say…"

"So, please keep this to yourself. I'll tell him when I'm ready. I know there's stuff he's keeping from me too. It's not like this is a one-way street."

Christopher finally picked up his sandwich and took a bite. "Fine. Whatever."

That was the most I was going to get out of him. "Thank you."

"But we need to figure something out with Hank," he said. "Maybe you should move your office."

"Like I can afford to just move my business."

He finished half his sandwich in a few bites, obviously starving since we spent most of our lunch hour yelling. "No offense, but your business isn't really a business. You don't make shit, and the company is hundreds of thousands of dollars in debt. Maybe you should just walk away from it."

"And do what?" I asked. "That place is my life."

"I'd bet my right hand Calloway would give you a job in a heartbeat."

He would. There was no doubt about it.

"You can do what you love and actually make a living while doing it."

I shook my head. "I could never ask him for a handout."

"Why not? He wouldn't mind."

"I'm not with Calloway because he's rich and wealthy. I like him for him—nothing else."

Christopher rolled his eyes. "That's not what this is about. And he knows that."

"He offers me a lot of things, but I never take them because I respect him too much. If I asked him for something, it would seem like I'm using him. And if I really want a job, I can apply for one all on my own."

"His company rejected you twice," Christopher reminded me. "Still not sure how a Harvard graduate gets ignored, but whatever."

"Education isn't important to Calloway. He never went to college."

"He didn't?" he asked, intrigued. "That's so cool. He built that company all on his own?"

I nodded.

"Badass," he said. "I wish I could be like him."

"You are like him," I reminded him.

"Not really," he said. "I work for a boss. I get a commission. I have business hours. Not Calloway. That guy can do whatever the hell he wants, when he wants."

"One day, you'll get there. Building an empire takes time."

"Anyway," Christopher said, picking up the other half of his sandwich. "You should ask him. If you aren't going to tell him the truth about Hank, you should at least do this. He may not realize it, but he'll be grateful when you work in a huge building around other people so Hank can't just waltz in there whenever he feels like. You're totally vulnerable in that tiny little office."

I knew I was vulnerable even with a bat behind my desk. There were no witnesses in the office. If Hank really had the energy, he might be able to pin me down. And I couldn't afford a security system for surveillance.

"Seriously, think about it. Hank can't touch you as long as you're living with me or Calloway. And he can't touch you at work either if you're at Humanitarians United. It's the best solution to get Hank to leave you alone."

I knew he was right—and that was saying something.

"You'll think about it?" he pressed. "Because I'm not gonna let this go until you make a decision—a smart one."

"Yes," I whispered. "I'll think about it."

4

CALLOWAY

T he second I walked through the door, pain crashed down on my body.

She wasn't there.

I missed having her at my house every day, smelling dinner the second I walked inside. I usually spotted her before she noticed me, standing at the counter with her back turned to me. Her ass was firmer than a nectarine, and it looked amazing in the denim jeans she always wore. Sometimes, she hummed under her breath, not even aware she was doing it.

But now I walked into an empty house.

I set my satchel on the entry table then flicked on a couple lights. My body collapsed on the couch, and I stared at the blank TV screen, listening to the silence. Traffic and people were completely blocked out. With my small backyard, it didn't feel like I was living in the city at all.

I pulled out my phone and texted her, my fingers hitting the screen harder than I meant to. My desperation was getting the best of me, and my hands ached to touch her. My sleeping pattern had been completely thrown off because she wasn't beside me every night. When I arranged for her to move in with Christopher, I thought it was the best idea. But now, I regretted the decision. *I want you.* It was the first thing that came to mind. Despite how intense the statement was, it was exactly how I felt—in as few words as possible.

Then come and get me. Her sassy voice could be heard when I read the sentence. Her green eyes would be lit up in flames, beautiful and hypnotizing. I pictured her standing in just a black thong, ready to crawl on the bed with her ass in the air.

Careful, Vanilla. You know I'll do it.

I'm making dinner with Christopher. I can come by later, unless you want to join us.

If I went over there now, I wouldn't get any sex. Christopher would want to talk about sports and women, and I'd barely get a few words in with Rome. But the idea of sitting around and waiting for her seemed terrible.

I'd miss her the whole time.

I'll be there in fifteen minutes.

See you then, Sexy.

Christopher opened the door. "Hey, man." He shook my hand firmly before he invited me inside. "It's been a while since I've seen you. What's new with you?"

"Just work and your sister." Rome was my favorite hobby, one that I never got tired of. I turned to see her standing in the kitchen, her face lit up with a smile just for me. I wanted to go to her immediately, but Christopher continued talking.

"So, you're rich, but you run a nonprofit," he said. "Where does your money come from?"

It was a nosy question, but I knew he was only asking because he was a financial advisor. He was merely curious. "I own a lot of real estate in prime locations in the city. Mostly commercial buildings and condominiums. My personal salary is an accumulation of all those things."

"What about depreciation?"

The last thing I wanted to do was talk about business. "I'm gonna say hello to my lady. But we can continue this conversation when I'm finished." I patted him on the shoulder so my brush-off wouldn't seem too rude.

He nodded his head slowly then winked. "I understand you, man."

I closed the gap between us, slowly getting closer to Rome until I could finally smell her. The smile she gave me was enough to make me soften. My exterior didn't feel quite as hard. Normally, I felt like solid metal. But her flames were so scorching, she made me melt. "There's my woman." My arms circled her waist, and I kissed her softly on the mouth, not giving a damn if Christopher was looking. The second her lips were pressed to mine, I felt euphoric. She tasted like heaven, so sweet and ethereal. My hands tightened on her waist, and I continued the kiss longer than I should have—but I couldn't help it.

She was the one to break away first, biting her bottom lip like she wished the kiss could continue. She averted her gaze immediately, like she was embarrassed by the affection she'd just displayed in front of her brother. "Hope you're hungry."

My eyes were glued to her mouth. "Starving."

Rome picked up on my double meaning, her cheeks flushing slightly. I pictured her ass looking the same way, red from my palm. "Want a beer?" She retrieved a bottle from the fridge without waiting for my response.

"Sure." I twisted off the cap and took a drink.

"You can have a seat. Dinner will be ready in a few minutes."

I didn't go over there to spend time with Christopher in front of the TV, but whatever. "Need help with anything?"

"Nope." She turned back to the counter and continued slicing the vegetables.

I walked into the living room and sat on the couch, Christopher perched on the other one. "So, what were we saying?"

"All your thoughts fell out of your head when you looked at her, huh?"

I smiled before I took a drink. "Something like that."

After dinner, Rome entered the kitchen and washed the dishes.

Christopher talked to me about IRAs and other financial bullshit before he nodded toward the hallway. "There's something I want to show you."

"Where?"

"In my bedroom." He left his beer on the dining table.

I raised an eyebrow, not interested in entering another man's bedroom.

"Just come." He walked down the hallway with me behind him. Once we entered his bedroom, he shut the door behind us.

And that made things weirder.

He crossed his arms over his chest and faced me, keeping his voice down. "Alright, I wanted to talk to you about something without that pain in the ass overhearing."

Now I was interested. "What's up?"

"She's having some problems at work right now, and she needs to walk away from the business. She's been losing money for a long time, and keeping For All is doing more harm than good. I know she mentioned she applied to your company a few times but never heard back. I was wondering if you would give her a job."

I would give her anything she wanted. But why was I hearing this from him instead of her? "Why is this a secret?" Rome should trust me by now. There was nothing she could say to me that would upset me.

"Because she refuses to ask you for anything." Christopher rolled his eyes. "She doesn't want you to think she's interested in you for your money, wealth, and connections. So, she's stuck in this shitty situation until something better comes along. But nonprofit work that actually pays is slim pickings. She's gonna be in that shithole forever unless you give her a helping hand."

I processed everything he said, feeling moved about her priorities. She could ask me for help, but she refused to because I was too important to her. She valued our relationship more than making her life easier. Most women didn't care about me beyond my fucking skills, wallet, and empire. Her gesture meant more to me than I could ever put into words. With Christopher watching me, I kept my emotions below the surface, wearing my stoic expression like always. My thoughts were always a mystery to everyone around me—except Rome. "I'll take care of it."

"How?" he asked. "I don't want her to know I had anything to do with this."

"Don't worry about that. I'll take care of it."

He smiled and shook my hand. "You're the man. If you ever want to marry my sister, you have my blessing." He winked then opened the bedroom door and raised his voice so Rome could hear our conversation. "Yeah, the Dow is doing terrible right now. Might have something to do with the election. There are so many variables when it comes to the stock market that nothing is certain, you know?"

We entered the kitchen area, and I nodded along. "I agree."

Rome had just shut the dishwasher. "Do you guys ever talk about anything else besides finances? Like sports?"

"Actually, yeah," Christopher said. "We were just talking about how you could benefit from some cooking lessons."

Rome crossed her arms over her chest, giving a hateful look that was scary but borderline cute. "I'm not cooking you dinner again."

"Good." Christopher walked into the living room and snatched his beer off the dining table. "I'll have beer for dinner."

She rolled her eyes when he wasn't looking.

Now that dinner was finished and we were face-to-face, I wanted to get out of there. Every moment my dick wasn't deep inside her was wasted time. "Let's go to my place." I didn't ask her because it wasn't a request. Christopher was cool, but I wasn't interested in spending time with him. My interest in Rome was very specific. All these dates and dinners were only part of the plan to get what I wanted.

"Now?" she asked.

"Right. This. Second." I stared her down without blinking, amazed by the beauty of her green eyes. I couldn't wait until they sparkled for me while she came as she dug her nails into my arms.

When she bit her bottom lip slightly, just a mere instant that was nearly impossible to catch, heat soared up my throat and into my mouth. I wanted to breathe hard into her mouth and for her to listen to how much I wanted her. "Let me get my purse."

I smacked her ass gently as she walked past me. "Hurry."

The instant we entered the house, our lips were locked and our arms were tangled together. Clothes fell to the floor as we maneuvered up two flights of stairs, our mouths still moving together with desperation. Before we entered the bedroom, I managed to make her moan twice.

When her naked body hit the mattress, I climbed on top of her and separated her thighs with my knees. She was finally ready for me to take her. It was just her and me, and her naked body was ready for me to enjoy.

I wrapped her gorgeous legs around my waist and tilted her hips as my cock inched inside her. This was my favorite part, the beginning and not the end. Her eyes always lit up when I sank into her, and her pussy stretched noticeably, resisting the thick intrusion. Her tightness always reminded me of her innocence, that I was the only man ever to fuck her. Her slickness always greeted me with open arms, and the groan that escaped her voice was mixed with pleasure as well as pain.

Her hair cascaded around her and across the mattress, the brown locks in slight curls. She wore very little makeup, but I could see dark mascara around her eyes. Her eyelashes were thick and long, making her already beautiful eyes look majestic. Her nipples were hard and her chest was red, obvious signs of arousal. Her lips were slightly parted, the tip of her tongue sitting behind her teeth.

"You have no idea how fucking beautiful you are."

She ran her hands up my chest, feeling the solid slab of concrete. "Yes, I do. Because I see the way you look at me."

Naturally, my eyes softened. Her words were sweet and unexpected, and they somehow made me feel warm inside. For the first time, I didn't want to hurt her. Treasuring her, adoring her, and feeling her was enough.

Vanilla sex wasn't so bad—not bad at all.

I slid deep inside her until my balls hit her entrance, resting against her ass. My arms were locked on either side of her head, and I slowly began to thrust, rolling my hips as I slid in and out of her. Like a hand squeezing my length, she was tight. If she weren't so wet for me, this might not have worked.

Her hands snaked to my biceps, her fingertips curling around the muscle and her nails digging in. Slowly, she moved with me, using her legs as an anchor to reposition her lower body. When I slid inside her, she moved to take more of me. The possibility of pain never deterred her from having me. It didn't matter how big my dick was — she still wanted me.

This was what I'd wanted all day. When I was at work, I couldn't stop picturing her underneath me like this. There were no whips or chains, but it was still unbelievable. Only a woman like Rome could entertain me through sex as slow and gentle as this. One day, I would get bored of it. But for now, I was fully entranced.

"You make me come so fast…" Redness spread to her cheeks, her eyes darkening in pleasure.

"The feeling is mutual, sweetheart." My hands pinned hers to the mattress above her, dominating her as best I could. I thrust into her harder, giving her more of my length than she'd ever taken before.

Her fingers interlocked with mine, and her moans turned to screams. Her pussy clenched around me as she flew over the edge. Writhing and moaning, she came all over me, her pussy soaked and sheathing my dick in her juice. "Calloway...fuck." She rode the high for nearly a minute then bit her lip, looking into my eyes with pure satisfaction.

When she gave those amazing performances, I wanted to ride the same high, to give in to the most natural feeling in the world. But I wanted to see her eyes roll into the back of her head again, to hear those screams get louder.

I dug one hand into her hair and pressed my mouth against hers, my eyes still focused on hers. There was so much moisture between us that my cock moved with less resistance. My sheets would be covered with the lubrication that leaked down her ass and underneath her. But I loved feeling her arousal caked over my length. I loved pleasing my woman as much as she pleased me.

"Calloway...I want your come."

For being vanilla, she said the dirtiest things. "You want it, sweetheart?"

"Yes," she said through her heavy breathing. Her nails dug into mine, and she looked straight into my eyes, watching my expression just as I was watching hers. "I like watching you come..."

"How ironic. I love watching you." I thrust into her harder, crashing my headboard into the wall and nearly snapping it in two. My body pressed her into the mattress, rumpling the sheets with our movements. Sweat covered us both, but the sensation was worth every minute of the exertion.

I kissed her hard, bruising her lips with mine. Together, we breathed as one, taking as much of each other as we could. My mouth treasured her everywhere, moving to her neck and her succulent nipples. When my mouth touched hers again, she came once more.

The second I felt her tighten around me, I let myself go.

I locked my eyes with hers and came with a groan, releasing with her at the exact same time. I shoved my length deep inside her, wanting to make sure she got every single drop. There was nothing sexier than sleeping next to the woman I just pumped full of my seed.

She slowly came down from her high, her fingertips moving through my damp hair. Her ankles locked together, and it didn't seem like she wanted me to pull away anytime soon. Her nipples slowly softened, and the sweat on her chest looked lickable. "I wish we could do this all day, every day."

Those words lit me on fire once again. Instead of pulling out and hopping into the shower, I wanted to stay right there. "We can do this all night." I licked her sweat away, tasting the salt on my lips, and once again, I was hard.

She dragged her nails down my back, nearly slicing me open as I thrust into her again. "God, Calloway... Where have you been all my life?"

I kissed the corner of her mouth as I rocked into her. "Waiting for you."

<hr />

I met Rome for lunch.

Looking sexy as hell in a tight pencil skirt and a skintight pink blouse, she nearly made my jaw drop. Somehow, she looked just as sexy with clothes on as she did when they were on my bedroom floor. Her slender legs looked toned in the stilettos she wore. Absolutely breathtaking, she walked into that restaurant without any clue how many men were staring at her.

When she spotted me at the table, she walked over to join me.

I nearly forgot to rise to my feet to greet her. I was hoping she would sit in my lap instead. "Hey, sweetheart." I wrapped my arm around her waist and gave her a kiss that was considered PG.

"Hey, Sexy." That's how she always addressed me, and it was my favorite nickname I'd ever been given.

I pulled out her chair and sat across from her, all logic and reasoning going out the window. All I could think about was how perky her tits looked today. Her sexy bra made her rack look incredible. The hollow of her throat looked like it needed my tongue's attention. Actually, her entire body looked like it needed my attention.

"You always look at me like that." She grabbed the menu and lowered her gaze to read it.

I didn't pretend I didn't know what she was talking about. I owned up to it like a man. "Because I'm obsessed with you." What was the point in sugarcoating it at this point? Ever since she slapped me in that bar, I'd been hard up. It didn't matter how many times we fucked, or how much furniture we fucked on, I still wanted more of her.

"Every time you look at me?" She looked up at me again, her eyes flirtatious.

"And every time I'm not looking at you."

The corner of her lips rose in a smile.

"I'd fuck you right now if it weren't illegal."

"Too bad," she said. "I've always wanted to do it in a public place."

My eyes narrowed as she teased me. It was arousing, but that was dangerous for her. I could take her in the bathroom right now, not giving a damn who was in the next stall. "Careful, sweetheart. I'll make that happen right now if you keep this up."

The tension rose between us, palpable and scorching. Her leg moved to mine under the table, and she brushed up against me seductively, wanting my enormous cock inside her right then and there.

I did my best to ignore my raging hard-on in my slacks.

Fortunately, the waitress came to our table and dimmed the mood. Once the food and drinks were ordered, she left us alone.

I watched Rome's beautiful face, wanting to wrap her brown hair around my fist until I had a good hold on her. Fantasies came into my mind, each one of them involving rope, chains, and my palm. She was obedient, doing as I asked without hesitation. She didn't meet my gaze until I commanded her to. She only referred to me as Sir.

She could read my emotions, but thankfully, not my thoughts. "You're doing it again."

She didn't know the half of it. "There's something I need help with. And you're the perfect person to turn to."

"I'm not giving you a blow job in the bathroom. I'll admit I'm a little slutty with you, but I have some class."

I smiled, something so rare I nearly forgot how to

do it. This woman made me feel things I hadn't felt in decades. "What little class you have left is about to disappear. But that's not what I wanted to talk about."

"I'm listening." She adopted her professional composure, staring at me intently with open ears.

"The head of the Homeless and Working Class Department just resigned a few weeks ago." Actually, I just promoted her to a higher salary position two days ago. "I haven't found a suitable person to replace her and wanted to see if you were interested. The primary duties of this role are to orchestrate food and clothing drives for the homeless, as well as work to find them suitable jobs. The working-class aspect focuses on programs to aid underprivileged communities, single-parent families, etc. If you're interested, I'll write you a formal offer letter with your salary listed. With your experience and education, I truly believe you're the best person for the job." Rome was smart, compassionate, and no one would do a better job than her. There was no doubt her heart was in the right place, and frankly, she could help a lot more people with a bigger budget and team members.

First, she was shocked. Her mouth opened slightly at the incredible offer I just gave her. Her eyes lit up the same way they did when we were in bed together. But instantly, that delight changed to suspicion. "Did Christopher ask you to do this?"

I played dumb. "To get you to move out? He may have mentioned you were a little annoying, but no, he didn't ask me to offer you a job." I didn't have a problem lying when it came to someone else's privacy. "If you don't want it, you don't have to take it. I just thought I would talk to you about it because the position is open. I understand you're passionate about your company, so if you want to stay there, that's perfectly fine." The more aloof I appeared, the more likely it was she would consider the offer.

Her suspicion died once she heard everything I said. "I don't know what to say... I'm flattered."

"I'm not trying to flatter you, sweetheart." Although, I loved it when her cheeks turned red like that; it made my palm twitch under the table. "Does that mean you're interested?"

"Of course, I am." She chuckled as if the question were humorous. "I've been having some problems with For All lately, and I'm not sure if I can solve them."

I knew she had a scary amount of debt from student loans and running a nonprofit all on her own. Honestly, I was surprised she'd lasted this long. "I think you'll be able to help people just as much, if not more, with Humanitarians United. If you walk away from your company, you aren't abandoning the people you serve. You aren't abandoning this city or the community. I really think you'd be a great asset to the team."

She smiled in that beautiful way that went straight to my heart. "You're so sweet, Calloway."

I wasn't trying to be sweet. I was working to make her my submissive—the best submissive I would ever have. "Does that mean you accept my offer?"

She fingered her water glass without taking a drink. The glass was full of ice cubes, water, and a single lemon wedge. Condensation collected on her fingertips, reflecting the sunlight that came through the window. "I don't know…"

I hid my irritation deep in my gut, forcing myself to remain patient. "What's your hesitance?"

"You don't think it could be a problem? Us working together?"

If I had it my way, she would be bent over my desk every time I called her to my office. Her skirt would be bunched around her waist, and her panties would be around her ankles. Looking across the city, I would thrust into her and fill her with my seed, feeling like a king. "Why would it be a problem?" I fingered the black ring on my right hand, eager to slip the black diamond onto hers.

"Because we're seeing each other, Calloway. Won't that make people uncomfortable?"

"No one needs to know, sweetheart. And if it does make them uncomfortable, they can find another job."

She was warming up to the idea but still hesitant. "Are you sure about this? Maybe you need to take some time to think it over."

Nothing annoyed me more than someone doubting me. "I've been running this company for a long time. I believe I have the experience and capability to make important decisions on a daily basis." I didn't hide the anger in my voice. I didn't stop unclenching my jaw either. "No, I don't need to think it over."

She knew she'd crossed an invisible line. "I didn't mean to offend you."

"Then don't," I said coldly. "You want the job or not?"

Instead of answering right away, she sighed. "What if we have a fight? What if we break up?"

"Even if we have a disagreement, I'm sure both of us can remain professional at the office. And secondly, we aren't going to break up." The certainty didn't come from any belief in our relationship. It derived from obsession. There was no way in hell I was letting her walk away from me unless I was ready to let her go.

And I knew I wouldn't be ready for a long time.

"We aren't?" she asked quietly, her eyes soft.

I crossed my legs under the table, my hands resting together on my knee. She was a fiery opponent, someone who didn't settle for less than what she deserved. If she didn't agree with something, she had no problem voicing her opinion. "If you think I'd ever let you go, you're sadly mistaken."

5

ROME

I interrogated Christopher the instant I saw him. "Did you ask Calloway to give me a job?" I knew he didn't mention Hank. If he had, my conversation with Calloway would have played out quite differently. The table would have been thrown across the room, and there would be a story about Hank's murder on the prime-time news.

"What?" Christopher must have just gotten off work because he still had his tie around his neck. It was undone and loose, as were the buttons of his shirt. He had a beer in his hand as he sat on the couch, and his perfectly styled hair had started to come loose from the gel.

"Don't play stupid with me." I sat on the couch beside him and pointed my finger into his chest.

"Calloway offered me a job out of nowhere over lunch today. That's pretty random, don't you think?"

"Random?" he asked. "In case you've forgotten, both of you do the exact same thing for a living. It's not like he's a dentist and you're a gymnast. He's seen your work and knows you're good at what you do. Did that logic ever cross your mind?"

When my brother belittled me like that, I felt stupid for jumping to conclusions. "Sorry, I just thought it was strange that he offered me this amazing job out of the blue."

"People resign from positions all the time, and new people are needed to fill them... It's the circle of life. So, it's a good gig?"

"Yeah. I'll be the head of the Homeless and Working Class department."

"Cool," he said with a nod. "Sounds boring as hell to me, but good for you."

"How ironic. Your job sounds boring to me."

He shrugged. "It is pretty boring."

I chuckled. "At least you admit it."

"So, when are you moving out?" he blurted.

"I'm not moving out. You need someone to help with the rent, right?"

"Well...yeah." He drank his beer. "But I can always find someone else. If you want your space, you should get your own place. No hard feelings, really. Now that you'll have money, you should treat yourself."

"I have no idea what the salary is."

"I'm sure it's enough to live off of. Calloway seems like a guy who would pay his employees pretty well."

"Yeah." I just hoped I wasn't given special treatment.

"Having your boyfriend as your boss will be nice. You can get away with a lot of stuff."

I glared at him. "Like I would ever take advantage of that relationship."

"Why not?" he asked. "If I were screwing my boss, I would."

"I guess that's the difference between you and me."

"So, when do you start?"

"Not sure. I need to have a formal interview at his office tomorrow. He'll probably tell me then."

"Awesome. And what about For All? What are you going to do with that?"

Closing down the company wouldn't be that big of a deal. I only had a few part-time volunteers. It wasn't like they would be getting a cut in their paychecks. "I guess I'll cancel my lease and move my stuff out... pretty simple."

"Hank will have no idea how to track you down. Maybe he'll give up and forget about you."

"Yeah…" I hoped so. If not, I might have to kill him. I didn't put up with harassment. I'd tried contacting the police and that didn't work, but I would take the matter into my own hands if necessary.

I entered the large building and took the elevator to the top floor. Once the doors opened, I looked at the wide-open office space. Cubicles housed workers at their stations, typing away or talking on the phone. The perimeter of the floor contained offices, probably for the higher-up executives. It was obvious where Calloway's office was because the back of the building couldn't be seen at all, blocked by a black wall with a large desk sitting in front of it. Looking as if it was carved from stone sat an enormous desk with a pretty woman behind it.

I tried not to be jealous. Calloway didn't seem like the kind of man to sleep with an assistant.

"Hi." I walked up to her, feeling self-conscious once I was face-to-face with the pretty blonde. With perfectly flawless skin and blue eyes like Calloway, she was beautiful. "I have a meeting with Mr. Owens in fifteen minutes."

She looked up at me, showing the kind of smile a

model wore. It was disingenuous but perfect, displaying her straight teeth and a dimple in each cheek. Her blonde hair was so shiny the fluorescent lights glared off the top of her head. "Of course." Her fingers hit the keyboard until she found the right information. "Here you are." She turned back to me once she confirmed the appointment. "Take a seat, and he'll be with you shortly."

"Thanks." I sat down and crossed my ankles, feeling my heart pound when it shouldn't. I wasn't sure if I was nervous for the interview or just being alone with him. Last night, he took me from behind and wrapped my hair around his fist, controlling me like he was a cowboy and I was the horse. He came inside me so many times that I couldn't walk to the bathroom without dripping his seed everywhere.

The memory brought searing heat to my cheeks.

Excitement bubbled inside me, and I was suddenly eager to see him. I loved seeing him in a suit, his shoulders broad and powerful and his waist narrow and tight. His chin was usually sprinkled with a five o'clock shadow, rough to the touch when his face was pressed between my legs. Those eyes were the best, so scorching and intense.

I automatically squeezed my thighs together.

The large black door opened, and Calloway

stepped out, looking perfect in his crisp, gray suit. One hand was in his pocket, and his eyes were trained on my face like a target. He didn't smile with his mouth, but his eyes hinted at silent affection. "Ms. Moretti." He waited for me at the door, professional and borderline indifferent. But I knew it was all just an act.

I grabbed my purse and walked past him, aware of the scent of his cologne. The hairs on the back of my neck stood on end, tense from the heat in the air. I could practically hear the snap and pop of an invisible fire.

Calloway shut the door and blanketed us in complete privacy. He walked up to me, giving me no time to admire his office or the view. His face was close to mine, and he stared at my lips like they were his property.

I swallowed the lump in my throat, feeling the nerves get to me. I'd been seeing him for four months, but he still had this effect on me—the ability to make me squirm with need. I wanted to press my hands to his chest and feel that warmth and strength. Before I met him, I was so innocent. But now, all I could think about was moving our bodies together, making love that was so hot and sweaty I couldn't think afterward. That physical connection brought me to a new realm of existence. Spiritually connected, I felt something real with him. The sex was just an expression of those feelings—of desperation, affection, and so much more.

I knew what would happen if I didn't take control of the situation. My skirt would be above my waist, and I'd be getting fucked for the entire interview. It wouldn't be an interview at all. "Tell me more about the position." I walked around him and sat in the leather chair facing his desk. His desk was black like the bookshelves on the wall. His masculine tastes were obvious, looking similar to his home. The only brightness in his office came from the floor-to-ceiling windows.

He approached the front of the desk and leaned against it, crossing his ankles and his arms. The corner of his mouth was raised in a smile, amused by my obvious attempt to keep things professional between us. "You have more strength than I do." He tapped the surface of the wood. "You'd be on your knees right now if I didn't respect you so much."

A thrill ran down my spine, hitting me right between the legs. I pulled out my notebook along with a pen. After my thumb clicked the top, I pressed the tip to the paper. "If we're gonna work together, everything needs to be platonic between us at the office." I didn't want any of my colleagues to assume I only got the job because I was screwing Calloway. I wanted to be judged based on my own merits, not what I did with the boss. "We'll only be here eight hours a day. The rest of the time is ours."

"But if I have to watch you walk around the office — " He tilted his head as he examined my crossed legs. "Looking like that all day long, I'm gonna have a few slipups."

"Then maybe we shouldn't work together."

His smile dropped. "Vanilla, you need to loosen up."

"Or maybe I need to keep you in line." I tightened my legs together in response to the searing heat that burned at the apex of my thighs. When I couldn't have him inside me, I squeezed my thighs so tightly together that it helped me cope with his absence.

His amused grin was back. "I like the sound of that, actually."

We'd flirted back and forth long enough, and I was ready to get down to business. "Tell me about the job and what I'm responsible for."

After a long look, he walked around his desk and fell into the chair. When he sat behind the majestic piece of wood, he looked kingly. As if not just the building belonged to him, but the entire city. With his slightly messy hair, crystal blue eyes, and his charming smile, he was the ruler of the world. "A businesswoman. I like it." He opened a drawer and pulled out a folder. "Here's everything you need to know. You start Monday. Does that work for you?"

"Sure." I opened the folder and read the briefing. There was also an offer letter explaining my salary and benefits. When I looked at the number, I squinted because I wasn't sure if I was reading it correctly. "The salary…"

"Yes?" Calloway rubbed his fingers along his jawline, calm and suave.

"Is this right?" I held up the paper so he could see it.

"Yes. I know how to read, Ms. Moretti." He smiled in a condescending way, growing irritated when I doubted his reasoning. Obviously, he didn't like being told what to do.

"It just seems excessive. It's very important to me that I don't get any special treatment."

"You don't need to worry about that. Everyone gets paid the same here, whether you're an executive or a secretary. Makes no difference. But as you're promoted, you're given bonuses for years of service." He rested both of his hands on the desk, his fingers interlocked together.

"Really?" Now I was mesmerized by the offer he'd just made, moved beyond words. Calloway ran a company aimed at helping other people. But he also took care of the employees under his wing.

"Yes. With donations as well as investments made by the company, it allows Humanitarians United to offer a competitive salary. It makes a great working environment because people are passionate about their careers, and they also make enough to put food on the table."

Speechless, I stared at the paper. Even if I didn't still live with Christopher, I would make enough money to actually make payments toward my loans every month. Right now, I was only putting in a feeble amount and never taking anything off the principal. My bill wasn't getting any smaller, but I had to keep paying it every single month. With this job, I could finally eliminate my loans, one paycheck at a time. "I don't even know what to say…" I was used to living check to check—and sometimes not getting a check at all.

The longer Calloway watched me, the more his look softened. He tried not to pity me because I asked him not to, but the expression always slipped out. "You don't need to say anything. Just show up on Monday."

This was my dream job. It was something I wanted to do, and I'd never imagined making this kind of money. It was probably nothing to most people, but to me, it was like winning the lottery. "Thank you." Those two words didn't adequately express how much it meant to me. Now I could do what I loved without having to worry about Hank stopping by. If he came to my office inside Humanitarians United, Calloway would snap his neck.

"And if you're ever interested in making extra cash, I have a few side things you can do." He winked.

I smiled at his teasing nature, knowing he was only half joking. "This is more than enough, so I don't need anything else. But I'll gladly do those things for free." I winked in response.

His eyes lit up with joy, like it was Christmas morning. "Good answer, sweetheart."

I scrolled through the apartment listings on my laptop, trying to find a price that wasn't outrageous. I could afford a nice place on my own, but this was Manhattan, and real estate was insane.

Christopher walked behind the couch and spotted the listings on my screen. "Rome, what the hell?"

"What?" I asked without turning around. I continued to scroll, making mental notes about the listings that seemed like a good fit. The two things I cared most about were location and cost.

"You aren't moving out." He hopped over the back of the couch and landed beside me. His hand slammed on the top of my laptop, and he shut the screen. "You're stuck here, so don't even bother looking."

"I thought you were eager to get rid of me." I opened the screen again.

"Normally, yeah." He grabbed the screen again and shut it. "But not with Hank out there. He can track you down in an apartment. But if you're here, he can't mess with you. The only way you're leaving is if you move in with Calloway."

When I opened the screen again, I kept my hand on the edge so he couldn't close it again. "First of all, you don't tell me what to do. I'm not sure how you forgot about that. And second of all, I can't live with you forever. You have your life, and I have mine."

"Rome, I don't mind having you here. Honestly."

"I know. But we're both adults. We're too old to have roommates."

He grabbed the top of the screen.

This time, I growled through my teeth.

He quickly pulled his hand away like I might bite him. "As long as Hank is a problem, you either live with me or Calloway. That guy is dangerous, and we both know it. I'm not bossing you around, but we both know there's no other option right now. Unless you find a roommate that's a former member of the KGB or something."

"I think a member of the KGB would be more dangerous than Hank."

"Exactly," he said. "Hank would definitely back off."

All I needed was Calloway. With one look, Calloway would scare him off in a heartbeat. But I wasn't ready to take that road—not yet. If I told Calloway what had happened, he would be so upset that he wouldn't be able to see reason. Hank would end up in a dumpster somewhere on Long Island. "Alright, I won't move —for now."

"Good." He left the couch and headed into the kitchen to grab a beer. "So, are you nervous for tomorrow?"

"Yes." I would be lying if I said I wasn't.

"Did you wrap up things with For All?"

"Yeah, it was pretty easy." Actually, it was pathetic how easy it was to close down my business. I didn't have very many donors, and the ones I did have didn't have a lot of capital. My volunteers found other jobs within the snap of a finger. And I happened to be at the end of my yearly lease anyway. Now I had one less thing to pay for.

6

CALLOWAY

R ome was a tough cookie who could take care of herself. She'd experienced more adversity than most people I knew, and as a result, she stood tall on her own two feet. When someone tried to rob her, she pinned his ass to the floor and called the cops. She could handle living in rough neighborhoods because that's what she was accustomed to. She was proud, strong, and spunky.

Her only hint of innocence was her virginity.

Which I took—gladly.

But I was relieved she wasn't working in that tiny office underneath a Chinese restaurant in East Manhattan. Every time I walked inside, no one else was there. If a guy gave her a hard time, it wasn't like she could scream for help. She was handling a dying business all on her own, but she'd refused to walk away out of misplaced pride.

But now she would be working for me.

Truth be told, I thought she would be a great addition to the staff. Hardworking and compassionate, her heart was in this for the right reasons. She was grateful for the new salary, but money didn't mean anything to her.

Honestly, she should be the one running my company.

I looked forward to working with her every day. When we were in our respective offices, we wouldn't bump into each other often. And if I made an excuse to walk into her office every single day, people would immediately suspect what was going on.

But could I really keep my dick in my pants?

That was a hard no.

I usually got to work an hour later than the rest of the staff because I was up late at Ruin. When I dropped off Rome at her apartment, I swung by the club to check on things. As a result, I needed that extra hour of sleep before I hit the gym and went to work.

My secretary handed over my messages as well as my schedule for the day. I had a lunch meeting with one of our most charitable donors, so I wouldn't be able to sneak off with Rome. But it wouldn't hurt for me to pop into her office and say hello on her first day. So, when my secretary took her morning break, I planned to stop by.

I just had a feeling I would never leave.

Rome's office door was left open, so I stood in the doorway and stared at her. She sat behind the large mahogany desk with her MacBook open on the wood. A vase of flowers rested on the corner along with a pink mug full of an assortment of pens. A single picture frame sat on the surface, a picture of her and Christopher at Coney Island.

I took a moment to look at her, enjoying the view before she noticed me. My hands were deep inside my pockets as I leaned against the door frame, loving the way her tits shook slightly when she typed. Her hair was pulled back into a ponytail, and her strands were curled and soft.

She must have felt the heat of my stare because her eyes moved directly to my face, her dark eyelashes long and thick. She wore more makeup than she usually did, dark eye shadow around her eyes and red lipstick on her mouth.

I pictured lipstick stains all over the base of my cock.

When she noticed my presence, her body stiffened immediately. It was the same reaction she would give if she were scared. Her breathing hastened, and her chest rose and fell with the increased pace. Her lips were slightly parted, her tongue pressed against the inside of her bottom teeth. When she moved her head slightly, her ponytail swung like a pendulum. "Mr. Owens, how can I help you?"

Everyone at the office called me that, but when Rome addressed me in that way, I wasn't even sure if she was speaking to me. I walked farther into the office but didn't shut the door behind me—as much as I wanted to.

I sank into the chair across from her desk and crossed my legs, resting my ankle on the opposite knee. My elbows rested on the leather padding of the chair, and my fingers pressed against my jawline, the smooth skin already hardening with new hair. "Wanted to see how your first day is going."

She shut her MacBook and leaned back in her chair, the buttons of her blouse fastened all the way to her neck. So far, she'd made a good impression at the office. The rest of the team immediately noticed her good heart and how valuable it was. "Really good. I've been getting up to speed with everything on the calendar. I have to say, you guys get a lot of stuff done. At For All, I would have felt productive accomplishing a fraction of the work Humanitarians United does on a routine basis."

I appreciated the compliment. "Thank you. But we have a great staff here and lots of resources. Imagine what you can do now with a bigger budget and more teammates." If we had an employee of the month, she would get it—every time.

"I'm very motivated. I feel like I can really make a difference here."

I heard what she said, but my eyes fixated on her lips, watching them move. I wished we were at my place, making out on the couch. Her small tongue moving against mine before she sucked my bottom lip. When I would palm her tits, she'd moan deep into my mouth.

Now I was so fucking hard.

Rome picked up on the static in the air, feeling my desire even though I hadn't made a single advance. "If I have any questions, I'll let you know." She was dismissing me, trying to get me out of her office before her skirt was pulled above her waist and her panties were stuffed into my pocket.

I didn't move an inch, my eyes glued to her face.

Her cheeks began to flush, her natural response

when she was either aroused or nervous, and in this case, both.

She cleared her throat. "Is there anything else?" She forced her voice to remain strong, determined to ignore the heat between us. Professional office decorum was important to her, for whatever reason. But if I had X-ray vision and could see through that desk, I knew I'd spot her thighs pressed tightly together, wishing I were deep inside her at that very moment.

Without saying a single word, I rose out of the chair and buttoned the front of my jacket. I gave her one final look before I walked out, knowing she was staring at my ass as I left her office.

I had to keep my hands to myself while we were at work.

But when we were at my place, that mouth, pussy, and ass belonged to me—and only me.

Vanilla sex was good—for now.

But I felt my hands shake with anticipation, needing dominance and control. I couldn't stop picturing ropes bound around her slender wrists, the material chafing against the gorgeous skin. I couldn't stop imagining her ass in the air, her pussy slick and ready for me. Blindfolded and gagged, she'd be my plaything.

Eventually, I would come clean about what I wanted, and we could start our new relationship. If she gave it a chance, I knew she would adore it. She would want me to hit her harder then smack my palm against that gorgeous ass one more time before the fun was over.

But I needed to ease her into it.

If we went from vanilla to whips and chains, she'd push me away. Her lack of experience told me this would be more complicated, but at the same time, more fun. I had a few ideas to warm her up, to broaden her horizons and her way of thinking. To her, they would be huge steps. To me, they would be the gateway to all my fantasies.

I was sitting on the couch waiting for her when a knock sounded on the door.

I was still in my suit and tie, not wanting to change since I was going to take off all my clothes anyway. And I knew she liked the way I looked when I dressed like this, like the ruthless dictator that I was.

I opened the door and saw Rome in the same clothes she wore to the office. She hadn't stopped by her apartment to change because she wanted to get here as soon as possible, her resistance finally disappearing.

Without a greeting, I grabbed her by the wrist and pulled her inside. My foot hit the door to close it, and then I stared down at her like the prey she was. My hands moved around her waist then snaked down to her ass. I gripped both of her cheeks as I guided her to the couch, my mouth close to hers. I didn't kiss her, purposely teasing both of us until we were naked together, her pussy on my lap.

I unzipped the back of her skirt and heard it thud to the floor. Her top and bra came next, followed by her black panties. Just as I undressed her, she stripped my clothes away. She was a little aggressive with the tie, yanking on it harshly. But I liked her roughness. I wished she would do it more often.

I sat on the couch with my knees spread apart, my cock lying against my stomach. I tapped my thigh and silently commanded her to straddle me, to do as I wanted with no questions asked. I wanted to speak my mind, to control her like I did with all the others. But I kept my mouth shut and directed my desires with my eyes.

She straddled my hips with her heels still on, the shoes pressed against the outsides of my thighs. Once she was on top of me, I could feel the moisture from her pussy. I hadn't even kissed her yet, and she was wet.

I had a feeling she was wet all day at the office.

I pulled her close to me until our chests were touching. My hand snaked around her neck possessively, my fingers digging into her skin with restrained force. Then I brushed my lips past hers, preparing to dive headfirst.

She shivered at my touch, electrified by how good it was.

This woman made me want to come with a single kiss.

I pressed my mouth to hers and kissed her slowly, my cock still underneath her but not inside her. I slowly rocked my hips to move my hard length against her, to rub her sensitive clit and give her extensive foreplay. The warm-up was unnecessary because she was clearly wet—but I enjoyed it anyway.

I forced my hand to remain relaxed as it gripped her neck. I wanted to choke her slightly, to make her pant into my mouth in desperation for air. I'd choked Isabella many times—and it always made her come hard.

My free hand groped Rome's perfect tit, my thumb brushing over her nipple and making it pebble. Her hair was still in the ponytail, so I grabbed the hair band and yanked it so hard it snapped. Her soft hair fell around her shoulders and brushed against my knuckles, feeling like cotton.

My cock twitched in irritation, wanting to be inside the tightest pussy I'd ever felt. I shifted her hips and shoved my cock head inside her, squeezing through the soaked channel. I pulled her down until I was completely sheathed inside her, feeling that slice of heaven. "Fuck, Vanilla." I released her neck and gripped her ass cheeks with my palms, squeezing the powerful muscle as I guided her up and down my length.

Her hands held on to my shoulders for balance as she moved with me, her tits shaking every time she lowered herself entirely on my length. The sexiest moans escaped her lips, her eyes bright and vibrant in ecstasy.

I moved with her, grinding slowly because the simple sensation of feeling our bodies together was enough. My preference was to pound hard and fast, aggressive fucking that would make us both sore. But these slow and restrained movements were somehow better. And I suspected that had something to do with Rome.

I cupped her face with my hand, my fingers brushing against her brown strands. My thumb moved across her bottom lip as I kept my forehead pressed to hers, breathing through the pleasure together.

I slipped two fingers into her mouth, placing them

on her tongue. "Suck." My authoritative tone emerged, but I couldn't keep it back. When I was in my element, my true colors always came out.

She did as I asked, closing her mouth around my fingers and sucking them. She gripped my fingers between her tongue and the roof of her mouth, giving pressure that was soaked with saliva.

I forgot to thrust into her because I was mesmerized by what she was doing with that sexy mouth of hers. She hit nerve endings that I'd never really paid attention to. The natural way she listened to my commands made me believe this could really happen — that she would eventually be tied up inside of Ruin.

I pulled my fingers out of her mouth then kissed her hard, my inner monster coming out to play. My hands returned to her voluptuous ass, and my fingers moved to her back entrance, wanting to steer her away from vanilla and to something much darker.

She kissed me with the same passion but immediately tensed when she felt the pressure of my fingers. "What are you doing?" She spoke against my mouth, her lips moving with mine.

I didn't pull my fingers away. "Feeling you."

Her pussy was still wet and tight around my length, but she grabbed my arm like her strength could outweigh mine. "I'm not into that."

I wanted to take this further, to show her a world she would fall in love with. But her hesitance to this new experience concerned me. If she couldn't do something so simple, she would never let me whip her. "Have you ever tried?"

She slightly rocked her hips, still keeping me inside her. "No…"

"Then how do you know you aren't into it?" I slipped my finger inside her ass again, saliva lubricating my penetration.

She scooted forward and away from my finger. "It's an exit only."

I wrapped my arm tightly around her waist and hooked her close to my chest. After a gentle kiss on the mouth, I spoke. "Whatever reservations you have, forget about them. I've never done anything that didn't make you feel good. Trust me to give you new experiences. Trust me to make you come for me." I kissed the corner of her mouth and didn't pull my fingers away, knowing she would allow me entry.

She continued to take my hard dick slowly, her moisture pooling around the base of my cock and my balls.

"Sweetheart." Despite my frustration, I remained patient. If I couldn't get her to do this, then there was no way I could convince her to be my sub. "I need you to trust me."

"I do trust you," she blurted.

"Then prove it." I thrust into her from below, my cock sliding in and out of her tight slit. I locked my eyes on hers, silently commanding her to obey me.

Something I said must have changed her mind because she finally agreed. "Okay."

The excitement in my chest didn't come from getting what I wanted. It came from the sense of hope that hit me hard in the gut. My instinct about her was right. I could train her to be the perfect submissive—all in good time.

I kissed her as I slid my forefinger through her opening, feeling her body reject me in the beginning. She was tense and nervous, her body unwilling to let me in even though she'd already verbally consented. I breathed into her mouth as I continued to work her ass. "Relax, sweetheart. You can always tell me to stop."

Gaining the control in the situation finally made her come back into the moment. Her fingertips dug into my shoulders as she kissed me again, allowing me to insert my finger deeper into her ass. Her channel was dangerously tight, much tighter than her pussy. When the time came for me to fuck her in the ass, we might have some problems.

We moved together, my cock stretching her over and over. When she became accustomed to my finger in her ass, she finally became passionate again, kissing me harder and digging her nails into my skin. I moved another finger inside her, stretching her wider apart.

She moaned into my mouth at the intrusion, struggling with the polar emotions. It was an unusual sensation, to be fingered in a place she had never touched, but at the same time, she clearly enjoyed it.

And when she enjoyed it, I enjoyed it.

"Sweetheart…" I wanted to come in her ass and her pussy at the same time. Unfortunately, that wasn't possible. I'd have to settle for her pussy for now and then her ass later.

"God…" Her lips pulled away from mine as she whimpered. "I'm gonna come."

I slid a third finger inside her, making it a tight fit. I forced her ass to stretch for my large fingers, pulsing inside her and feeling her tighten. "Come all over my dick, Vanilla."

She rolled her hips as she took my length several more times until her pussy clenched around me, squeezing me with a death grip. I fingered her harder as she came around me, her moisture pooling even more. "Calloway…"

I stared at her fiery green eyes as I approached my

climax, seeing the most beautiful woman in the world sitting on my lap. My fingers were in her ass, and my cock was impaled deep inside her. I had her wrapped around my finger—and she had me wrapped around hers.

I came with a violent release, overwhelmed with satisfaction. Memories of the first time I met her came back to me, when she'd strutted into that bar and slapped me with as much force as she could muster. I remembered the first time I kissed her, right outside her apartment door after the gala. I remembered the first time I fucked her and the drops of blood I found on my sheets afterward. Now we were getting down and dirty, going down a path of pleasure and pain.

I pressed my face into her neck as I finished, filling her pussy with every drop of seed I could produce. I wanted to make her feel full for the rest of the day, to feel a part of me inside her everywhere she went.

I slid my fingers out of her and leaned back, the remaining sensations of pleasure drifting away. Like I was on a cloud, I felt an intense high that made me float in the air. When Rome did the things I liked, it was impossible for me to truly grasp it.

Her hands slid to my chest, rubbing the sweat that had formed on the skin. She took time to catch her breath, her movements slow and even.

"So?" I asked a question I already knew the answer to.

Her lips remained tightly shut, her eyes telling me she had no intention of saying a word to me.

"I told you you could trust me." I'd done everything she'd asked of me up until that point, going on dates and bringing her flowers. I even let her sleep in my bed. Most surprisingly, I told her about my former demons when I'd never shared that information with anyone else. I bent over backward for this woman, and I'd earned her confidence.

"I'm not sure if I liked it, or if I just liked how much you liked it."

"Both, I'm sure." I pulled her next to my chest and gave her a soft kiss on the mouth. "I want to explore everything with you, Rome. I hope you let me."

She pressed her forehead to mine and looked down at my lips. Her nails dug silently into my chest, like she wanted more of me even though we were both satisfied. A strand of hair came loose from behind her ear and fell in front of her face. "I'm sure I will, Calloway."

Eventually, Rome and I would have the relationship I craved. Right now, I needed to continue earning her trust while exploring new realms of pleasure. One day, she would agree to be my sub, to trust me enough to start a new kind of relationship—one that was completely foreign to her.

So I forced myself to be patient with her.

And that kept my darkness at bay. I didn't bring out the chains or the cable ties. I didn't spank her hard when she was on her hands and knees. Slowly but surely, I would get us to the next level.

After dinner, we went to bed. When she was next to me, I slept better than usual, so I preferred to have her around. I wore my boxers, and she wore one of my t-shirts before we got under the sheets. Her arms immediately hooked around me like I was a stuffed teddy bear. Her leg hooked over my waist, and she cuddled into my side, stealing all the warmth from my body.

I loved it.

With her skin so soft and her smell so fragrant, it was like having a rose petal beside me. Her legs, smooth and silky, brushed against mine as she got comfortable. Sometimes her hair would brush against my shoulder, so soft and delicate. I wanted to fist it all night long, but then neither one of us would get any sleep.

I stared at her as she closed her eyes, looking like a queen. Her makeup was gone, and her natural features were on display for me. She had plump lips, the kind I loved to suck into my mouth. Her teeth were perfect and straight, sexy and adorable. As she started to drift away, I was even more awake. I would much rather watch her all night than get any sleep.

She must have felt my stare because she opened her eyes. "Yes?" She ran her hand down my back, her nails lightly scratching me.

I brushed my fingers along her cheek, expecting her not to be real because she was too perfect.

She watched me with lidded eyes, sexier than any other woman I'd slept with.

"You're so beautiful, it hurts." I stared at her lips, seeing my thumb rest on the corner of her mouth. "It hurts so much..." My chest ached as I examined her perfect features. She had a slender and elegant neck, reminding me of the grace of a queen. I'd sprinkled enough kisses in the hollow of her throat, but I never wanted to stop. Just when I thought I'd had enough of her, I wanted more.

An unfamiliar look came into her eyes, a quiet expression. Her hand moved up my chest until she reached my cheek. Her fingers glided over the skin until her fingertips rested on my bottom lip. She felt the softness before I kissed her fingertips, loving the way she explored me. She didn't say anything, but the look in her eyes showed more of her soul than she'd ever let me witness before. Wild and strong, she was a warrior underneath that petite frame. She'd suffered more than most, but she still considered herself to be lucky. She was remarkable, special. "When I'm not with you, everything hurts." Her hand moved back to my chest where it rested over my heart.

The nightmares were less frequent, but they still came every now and then. Rome was my dream catcher and chased them away with her natural light. But tonight, her presence wasn't strong enough to defeat my demons.

I dreamt of my father.

And my mother.

My father did a lot of terrible things in his life. Keeping women as submissives was one of the worst for a very big reason—because they were slaves. They couldn't escape, not without retribution. My mother was heartbroken, her husband choosing to be serviced by whores rather than by the woman he once vowed to love monogamously forever. When she threatened to leave, he threatened to hurt her.

He was a dictator, silencing everyone with terrifying

punishments. If we ever spoke out against him, tried to help the women he kept captive, we would experience a beating with a steel pipe.

In the middle of the night.

I remembered the sound the metal made when it crashed against my skull. Like the sound of metal on metal, it reverberated in my memory. Twelve all over again, there was nowhere for me to run or hide.

He chased me all through the house, taunting me for freeing one of his women.

I knew what would happen when he caught me.

I launched up in bed, the covers falling off of me as I gasped for breath. Drenched in sweat that traveled all the way down the back of my neck, I was scorched with heat. But once I was awake, the coldness got me. I felt sick, faint. I gripped the sheets to remind myself where I was—that my father was six feet under.

"Calloway." Rome pressed her chest to my back, her slender arms circling my waist. The smell of roses and fresh-cut grass washed over me, hinting of sunlight and doves. My breathing was still haywire, but her comfort made my heart rate drop by twenty beats. My hand gripped her wrist automatically, needing to know she was really there. "It was just a dream," she whispered. "You're here with me at 3:15 a.m. on Tuesday. You have work in just a few hours—so do I. You're a powerful man, and no one can touch you." She pressed a kiss to my back, right along my spine. Her lips were soft and loving, chasing away the remaining visions behind my eyes.

I'd never been so grateful to have someone there.

I'd never been so comforted.

Normally, I would head into the kitchen and deplete my storage of whiskey and scotch. But that solution couldn't compare to this one. My fingers remained wrapped around her tiny wrists, feeling her fluttering pulse. Curtains covered the windows, so it was dark in the bedroom. My eyes adjusted to the dimness, and I could see the faint light coming from the crack of the bathroom doorway. Rome's dress and heels were on the floor at the foot of the bed.

"I'm here." She scooted closer to me and pressed a kiss to my shoulder. She used her tongue this time, wetting my warm skin.

I closed my eyes at the touch, aroused and moved by the affection. I had spent nearly seven years sleeping alone, but she walked into my life and changed all of that. I was grateful she'd made me reconsider my ways. I wanted her more than I ever had, wanted to take her roughly against my mattress with her legs wrapped around my waist.

And that's what I did.

I grabbed her and positioned her back on the bed. My boxers were kicked off, and her panties were ripped in half. I crawled on top of her and widened her legs, dominating her and taking what I wanted.

Rome didn't object, her arms hooking around my neck.

I shoved myself inside her and rocked into her hard, thrusting and moaning. The cold sweat on my body was replaced with new drops from my exertion. I fucked the anger and pain out of my body, using Rome to forget about that nightmare.

I replaced my sorrow and sadness with pleasure. I replaced my loneliness with affection. I used Rome to feel good, to feel alive rather than dead.

Her green eyes were bright despite the darkness. When she gripped my forearms, she dug her nails into me. After a minute of screwing her, she was wet like usual, enjoying being roughly taken in the middle of the night. Maybe she was just doing it for me in the beginning, but now, she was doing it entirely for herself.

7

ROME

Calloway never talked about the nightmare he had—and that was fine. His reaction was much better than the impulse he used to have, which was to get so wasted he passed out and forgot the nightmare altogether. He didn't push me away or tell me to leave him alone. He let me wrap my arms around his body and hold him until the panic passed.

He told me his father used to be a violent maniac with cruel approaches to punishment, but he never went into the details of his childhood. I suspected there were more problems than he let on if he was still having nightmares as a grown man.

But I refused to ask because he would tell me when he was ready.

The following morning, neither one of us said much

to each other. Calloway was distant, but not cold, his mind somewhere else. He did his daily routine of showering, shaving, and then drinking a cup of coffee before he left for work.

Since we worked at the same place now, I had to wait inside his house for a few minutes before I left, just in case anyone found it suspicious that we arrived together every single day.

I didn't care what anyone thought of me. I pursued what I believed in and left the haters behind. But this was an entirely different situation. If my teammates didn't take me seriously, I wouldn't be able to accomplish all my goals. It was important for me to earn their respect. The second they knew I was screwing the boss, all my integrity and credibility would go out the window. They would assume I only got the job because I got under him every night—and on top of him.

We had a meeting that afternoon, working through lunch, and it was the first time I'd had to interact with Calloway in front of other people. I knew I could behave myself. I just hoped Calloway would do the same. He didn't care what the office thought of his personal life—but he didn't have anything to lose.

I walked into the conference room and purposely didn't look at Calloway. Lunch was set up in the back, an Italian meal with fettuccini and salad. I put a few scoops of everything onto my plate and grabbed a water before I sat down—far on the other side of the room.

Even though fifteen feet were between us, I pressed my thighs tightly together and looked over my notes while taking a few bites of my lunch. Anytime we were in the same vicinity, I thought about him in inappropriate ways. Thankfully, my office was on the other side of the building and nowhere near his. I could actually think straight with the door closed.

"Hey." Dean took the seat beside me in a collared shirt and slacks. He was roughly the same age as I was. He left his job at another nonprofit in California before he moved to Manhattan. "I love lunch meetings because of the free food."

I chuckled. "Yeah, that makes two of us." I gave him a smile so I wouldn't appear to be rude then turned back to my lunch.

"I've been meaning to ask you something." He spread out his things on the table in preparation for the meeting.

"Sure." I assumed he needed help organizing a clothing drive for the schools in the inner cities of New York. That was his department, which focused on providing for school-age children that needed clothes, technology, and books.

"Are you free tonight?" He looked at me

expectantly, his handsome face full of confidence. He was a good-looking guy with a heart of gold, but I'd never paid much attention to him.

I could feel Calloway's gaze snap in my direction, the heat from his look searing right through my skin. Without seeing his face, I knew his expression was dark and absolutely terrifying. Jealousy was a subject we hadn't encountered just yet, but it was obvious he was incredibly possessive of me.

"To work on a budget plan?" I asked, hopeful I was jumping to the wrong conclusion.

"Actually, I've kind of had a crush on you since you started here last week. I was hoping you'd like to go on a date with me."

Dean was nice, respectful, and friendly. If I'd never met Calloway, I probably would have said yes. But now that Calloway was the man who shared my bed every night, it was hard for me to picture myself with any other man.

I spotted Calloway in the corner of my eye, his shoulders positioned toward the two of us. His fingers rested against his mouth, blocking the crushing way he clenched his jaw. His eyes were trained right on Dean, prepared to rip his head off.

I pushed through the conversation so Calloway

wouldn't stab Dean through the eye with a pen. "You're so sweet, Dean. But I'm seeing someone."

"Oh…" He hid his disappointment with a curt nod. "I guess I should have known. You're such a beautiful—"

"Let's get this started." Calloway rose to his feet, looking terrifying with his squared shoulders and clenched hands. His pitch-black suit matched his sour mood, and he maneuvered to the front of the room with an alarming grace. He opened his folder on the table then rose to his full height, his tempered eyes immediately landing on Dean. "Where are we in the budget plans? I asked you to put them on my desk this morning, but yet, they are nowhere to be found."

Oh no.

Everyone sitting at the table flinched slightly at the anger in their boss's voice. They glanced at Dean, hoping their coworker had a good answer.

I had a feeling Dean was going to get fired today.

Dean was just as shocked by Calloway's hostility as everyone else. He watched his boss with trepidation before he finally opened his folder and looked through his things. "I just thought I would wait until the meeting—"

"I don't care what you think, Dean." With both hands on the table, Calloway leaned forward and stared him down. "I'm your boss, so if I ask you to do something, you do it. You think you know how to run this company better than I do?"

"Uh..." Dean stumbled before he found the right answer. "No, I just—"

"Just, what?" Calloway's ice-cold eyes stared into Dean's, combustive and nuclear.

This was bad—really bad. "Mr. Owens." I paused and waited for Calloway to meet my gaze.

After a heartbeat, he did. His gaze wasn't as threatening when he looked at me. It was slightly soft, the same expression I saw when he screwed me with both aggression and passion.

"Dean just told me he had some technical difficulties, so he wasn't able to get the budget report printed. He actually came to my office to use my computer, but I was having the same problem." I wanted to save Dean before he lost his job, and I wanted to counteract Calloway's rage. If I didn't put out his fire, he would burn everyone to ash.

Calloway stood up straight, some of his senses coming back to him. He didn't say another word on the subject and moved on. "Vanessa, where are we on the new donors?" He crossed his arms over his chest and looked at her, slowly returning to his calm self.

Now that the attention was off Dean, he sighed in

relief. "Thanks. I've never seen him act that way. And I've been here for years."

"He must be having a bad day," I whispered, unable to come up with a better excuse for a grown man having a tantrum.

"A really bad day," Dean said. "I'll make sure I don't cross him again."

That was definitely the smart thing to do.

I went home after work, finding Christopher on the couch playing a video game.

"Yo," he said without looking at me, his fingers hitting the buttons sporadically.

"Yo," I said back. "Calloway flipped out at work today."

"Why?" He paused the game. "Because you suck at your job?"

"Ha," I said sarcastically. "You're funny." I sat on the other couch and slipped off my painful heels. "One of my coworkers asked me out in front of Calloway."

"Uh oh," Christopher said with a chuckle.

"Calloway flipped out and nearly fired him. I had to redirect the conversation so Calloway wouldn't be a complete ass."

"Did he tell the guy you two were dating?"

"No," I answered. "But he yelled at him about something related to work...even though his anger had nothing to do with work."

Christopher seemed amused more than anything else. "Man, that guy has it bad. I hear wedding bells."

"I don't know about that..." I didn't mind the idea of spending forever with Calloway, but I was still annoyed with that little performance during our meeting.

"If a guy gets that jealous, then he's head over heels. Trust me."

"You don't know anything about relationships."

"Exactly. I've never been jealous over one of my ladies. I slept with this girl named Jessica, and the next day, I saw her on a date at a bar. Do you think I cared? Nope. Couldn't care less. When a guy does care, you know it's real."

"So, I'm supposed to think that was sweet?"

He shrugged and unpaused the game. "It's better than him not caring, right?"

"I don't mind that he cares. I just —"

A knock on the door stopped me in mid-sentence.

Christopher paused the game again and smiled. "Wow. Wonder who that could be?"

I rolled my eyes and answered the door, spotting

Calloway on the other side as I expected. In his black suit, he still looked angry, like I was somehow responsible for what happened that afternoon.

I refused to speak first, so I stared him down.

And he did the same back to me.

Christopher picked up on the tension and turned off his game. "I'm gonna take a shower..." He walked down the hall and shut his bedroom door, giving us some privacy.

Calloway didn't take his eyes off me once. "Can we have this conversation at my place?"

"Depends." I crossed my arms over my chest. "How is this conversation gonna go?"

He clenched his jaw when I didn't blindly follow him. "Some arguing. Some apologizing. And then some really good make-up sex."

"Who will be the one apologizing?"

"That remains to be seen." He backed out of the doorway. "But sex is guaranteed, and I don't want to fuck you hard when your brother is in the next room. So, let's go."

The only reason why I complied was because of the last part. Regardless of how annoyed I was, I always wanted good sex from him. It was better than yoga, a hot cup of coffee from my favorite bakery, and brunch with a friend on a Sunday.

We walked to his place a few blocks over, neither one of us saying a single word to each other. His hands were in the pockets of his coat, and he ignored the looks every passing woman gave him. Normally, he'd place his hand on the small of my back when he guided me across an intersection, but he refrained from touching me.

Once we were inside the house, away from prying eyes, he turned on me. "I know I got out of hand with Dean, but he shouldn't have crossed me like that."

"Crossed you?" I took off my jacket and hung it on the coat rack. "Calloway, he doesn't even know we're seeing each other. How was he supposed to know? Besides, he backed off when I told him I was seeing someone. Honestly, he's a pretty nice guy. Just because he asked me out doesn't make him a criminal."

"It does when it's my woman he's asking out." He clenched his hands by his sides like he wanted to punch something. His eyes were cold like icicles, just as they were earlier that afternoon. His five o'clock shadow made him appear more threatening.

For some reason, I found that sexy. I was annoyed with him, but I wanted to jump his bones at the same time. "You handled that situation horribly. I suggest you don't let it happen again. Your employees really respect you. Don't ruin that."

He closed his eyes for a moment, his temper fading away. "I know they do."

"Then you better apologize to Dean."

"I'm not gonna apologize to him. But I'll work to keep my temper under control. That's the best I can do."

I knew that was all I would get out of him. "Chances are, someone is gonna ask me out during the course of this relationship. And I know women probably ask you out all the time. We have to tune it out and keep moving forward."

"They better not." His anger made a resurgence. "If any man asks you out again in my presence, he's dead." He undid the front button of his jacket and tossed it on the couch. "This is all new to me. I've never been jealous before. I'm handling it the best way I can—even if it doesn't seem that way."

"It doesn't."

He sat on the couch, his long legs stretched out before him. He loosened his tie with one hand and stared at me. "If you watched a woman hit on me, you'd go insane too. Don't act like you wouldn't."

"I would." Without ever experiencing it before, I knew I would be ticked. "But I wouldn't flip out the way you did. I know you're faithful to me, so there's no reason to be angry." I slipped off my heels then kneeled before him at the foot of the couch.

His eyes watched my movements carefully. "I don't even look at other women. Just you."

I undid his slacks and pulled them down with his boxers, revealing his hardening cock.

His hand immediately went to my hair, getting a fistful of it within his fingers. He pulled back my head slightly just to tighten the grip.

"Let me make it up to you." I lifted the base of his cock and licked his balls, feeling the rough texture with the surface of my tongue.

He closed his eyes and moaned under his breath, his chest rising as he sucked in air.

I sucked one ball into my mouth while I massaged his length, which was now hard as steel. A drop of pre-come oozed from his tip and dripped down his length, meeting my tongue at the bottom.

Calloway opened his eyes and ripped off the tie around his neck. Then he did something I didn't anticipate. He pinned my wrists behind my back and tied them together with his soft tie, making a knot within five seconds that kept them bound together.

He scooted me backward then rose to his feet, his slacks and boxers hitting the floor.

I didn't know what was happening, but I liked it. I

liked sitting on my knees with my hands tied behind my back. His cock hung in front of my face, twitching in anticipation before he entered my mouth.

He looked down at me with hunger in his eyes. His hand reached for his base, and he pointed the tip against my mouth. He circled the head around my lips, tracing the outline like lipstick. "You're mine, Vanilla." He pressed his tip in the crack of my lips then pushed through, my jaw naturally opening for the girth of his cock.

He gripped me by the back of the neck as he thrust into my mouth, pulling me inward so his cock could reach my throat every single time. He fucked my mouth aggressively, his other hand resting on my shoulder so I could remain balanced on my knees. "I'm the only man who fucks this mouth."

I flattened my tongue so his cock could slide over the rough surface, picking up more saliva before he hit the back of my throat. My gag reflex was initiated a few times, but I fought against it, wanting his cock more than anything else. I felt my pussy soak my panties as mounds of saliva dripped from my mouth and down my chin. Tears sprang from my eyes because his cock was so big.

But I loved every second of it.

"You look so beautiful with my cock in your

mouth." He moved his hand to the back of my head and thrust deeper, fucking my mouth harder than he fucked my pussy. His length was like a steel rod, hard and straight.

He was the one who looked beautiful. Standing over me with his large height and powerful physique, he reminded me of a god. The muscles of his stomach clenched every time he thrust his hips. His biceps flexed as he pulled my mouth onto his cock. His expression was the best part. He looked so aroused that his lips parted, enjoying every sensation my throat and tongue gave him.

I wanted to come, but I knew he would give me what I needed once he was finished. I wanted to feel his come in my mouth anyway.

Calloway moaned quietly then stopped his movements, his cock still resting on my tongue. "Suck my tip."

I did as he commanded, sucking the head of his cock until I got every drop of his lubrication.

He pulled his hard cock out of my mouth. "On the couch, ass in the air."

I didn't think twice about it. Without the use of my hands, I fell forward on the cushions, my hands still bound behind my back with the silky tie keeping my wrists pinned together. My pussy was scorching, waiting for his cock to pierce me.

Calloway positioned himself behind me and grabbed the fabric of the tie between my wrists. Without warning, he shoved his massive cock inside me, giving my body no time to prepare for his girth. He yanked my hands so my back arched in a strained way. Then he pounded into me without mercy. "Mine. Do you understand me?"

All I could do was moan.

"Do you understand me?" he said with more authority.

"Yes," I said with a moan, enjoying his hard length moving deep inside me. I was just about to come when he stopped.

He pressed his lips against my ear, breathing hard. "Sweetheart, I'm not gonna let you come until you tell me what I want to hear."

Every second he didn't move inside me was torture. I needed that release. I needed to come all around him. If I didn't get it, I would go insane. "I'm yours, Calloway. Only yours."

He kissed the shell of my ear then breathed into my canal. "You're right about that, sweetheart. And what else?" He moved slowly, teasing me.

I didn't know what else he wanted me to say, so I

blurted out my first instinct. "And you're mine. All mine."

He shoved himself completely inside me, giving me every inch. "Yes." Then he pounded into me hard, driving into an orgasm that was explosive and powerful. Every inch of my body felt the unstoppable pleasure. It was so good I nearly forgot to breathe. The sex was rough enough to leave me sore the next day, but it was worth every second. His mouth returned to my ear again. "Ready for it, sweetheart?"

"Yes," I said with a pant.

"Here it comes." He gave his final thrusts before he inserted every inch deep inside me, depositing his seed and filling me to the brim. Some of his come spilled over and dripped to the cushion below me. When a moan erupted from his throat, I knew he liked his handiwork. "When Dean looks at you tomorrow, you're going to feel me inside you — even if I'm nowhere in sight."

Calloway sat on the couch beside me, reading a hardback while the TV was on. The volume was down so the basketball commentators couldn't be heard over the speaker. The fire in the hearth crackled and popped, bringing warmth to the living room.

I was doing paperwork beside him, wanting to be on top of all my responsibilities so I could impress the others. The easiest way to be accepted into a new team was by doing good work and not cutting corners. I could get away with almost anything since Calloway was my boss, but that type of behavior didn't interest me. The reason I took the job was so I could help people—not be lazy.

I became distracted when I noticed the knuckles of his hands. Veins ran over the back of his hands, protruding like thick ropes. They led up his forearm, which was chiseled with fine muscle. Every time he moved his fingers, they stretched and shifted under the skin. This man was so handsome that even his hands aroused me. They were so masculine, and I found myself wanting to kiss every knuckle.

Calloway noticed my stare, so he looked up, his beautiful eyes targeting me. In a black t-shirt and sweatpants that were loose around his hips, he looked like the cover of a *GQ* magazine. He didn't ask what I was staring at—at least not verbally.

"I like your hands," I explained.

"Thank you for the compliment," he whispered.

"I like this." I trailed my finger over a thick vein.

"Nurses like them too," he said with a quiet chuckle.

I didn't understand the comment, so I stared at him blankly.

"Easy to get in an IV," he explained. He turned back to his novel, his eyes following the words from left to right.

I wondered if that meant he'd been in a hospital. Although, if his father used to beat him, that answer was obvious. I turned back to my notepad and made some notes. After a few minutes, I felt his gaze burning into my cheek. I answered his look with my own.

He placed the ribbon between the pages as a bookmark before he closed the book. "You liked it when I bound your wrists together." He uncrossed his legs and spread his knees apart, his long legs stretched out onto the hardwood floor.

Since I couldn't tell if it was a question or an answer, I didn't respond.

"I'd like to do it again if you did."

I'd never had a man bind my wrists together—at least not in that context. I'd never had a man go anywhere near my ass either. But I found myself doing unorthodox things with Calloway—and liking it. "I did."

He moved his arm to the back of the couch and rested his fingers against the side of my neck. His fingertips touched strands of hair as he caressed me.

"There are other things I'd like to try with you too—if you're willing."

"Like what?" I knew couples did kinky stuff, like tying each other to the headboard and eating stuff off one another. They were things I never cared about, but after I met Calloway, I understood their appeal. "You want to handcuff me to your bed? Eat stuff off me?"

His eyes darkened as they focused on my lips. "Yes, among other things."

"I have an open mind." But I also wasn't that adventurous either. As long as it was tame, I'd be okay with it. It wasn't like Calloway was into the shit Hank used to be into. We'd only been dating for a short time when he demanded sex from me. When I said I wasn't ready, he tried to make it happen anyway. That was how I broke my arm—in two different places. Hank had specific interests sexually, like hurting me. I didn't find out about his tastes until I was admitted to the hospital.

"Good," he said. "I'm glad you finally trust me."

I didn't see what trust had to do with it. The moment I gave my virginity to him, my feelings were pretty clear. I knew Calloway was nothing like Hank or any of the evil men I'd encountered on my journey through life. I wouldn't have been sitting there beside him in that very instant if my heart wasn't already on the line. I was skeptical of a man this great, but my doubts went away long ago. "I trusted you a long time ago, Calloway. I know you would never hurt me, lie to me, or mislead me."

His fingers paused on my neck, and his eyes softened in a way they never had before.

Sometimes I wondered if I loved him. We'd only been seeing each other for five months, and that seemed far too soon to develop those kinds of emotions. But on the other hand, I noticed the way my heart always quickened when he was near. I noticed how well I slept when his massive body was beside mine. I noticed how happy I was when I saw his face first thing in the morning. Maybe it was too good to be true.

But maybe it wasn't.

Calloway pulled me into his side and pressed his lips against my temple. "You're my whole world, Rome." He left his mouth in place as he held me, the scent of his natural, masculine fragrance washing over me. "The way you make me feel... Sometimes it scares me."

"It scares me too."

He kissed my temple again. "I guess we can be scared together."

8

CALLOWAY

I was at Ruin doing the books that night because I hadn't made an appearance in over a week. Rome was the center of my universe, and naturally, I let my other responsibilities slip away. Jackson was too much of an idiot to be of much help, so everything fell on my shoulders. Thankfully, he wasn't there that night. If he were, he would have given me shit about Rome for an hour straight.

Christopher texted me, my phone lighting up with his name.

What did he want?

I swiped the screen and saw his message.

I need to call in a bro-code favor.

I'd never heard of such a thing. *I'm listening.*

I'm at the bar right now. I've got two women on the hook

who want to see my pad. This is my first threesome, and I CAN'T fuck it up.

You need me to teach you how to be with two women? I smiled just before I sent the message. My affection for Rome only grew the more I got to know her adoptive brother. I liked him a great deal, and he made my life so much easier.

Fuck you, asshole. I need you to get Rome out of the apartment. She said she was staying in tonight.

He'd never had a problem telling his sister to take a hike before. *Why don't you just tell her?*

Because she's my roommate. It's her home too. I can't kick her out whenever I want. It would be different if she was just crashing on my couch. And you owe me a favor, man. Whatever plans you have, cancel them.

Whoa, what? I don't owe you shit. Last time I checked, I hooked him up with a great apartment in a prime location. *You have a sweet apartment because of me.*

That I can't keep until she decides to move out. And it doesn't seem like she's leaving anytime soon. So, back to the original subject, can you take her out to dinner or something? Just get her out of my hair, alright?

I had no problem spending time with Rome. I was just caught up in a few things at Ruin. *I'll ask her to sleep over.*

Thanks. I need her out of there in thirty minutes. My ladies are ready to leave.

I'll do my best.

You'll get it done, man. We're talking about a threesome here. That's like the Nobel prize for pigs.

I rolled my eyes and shoved my phone into my pocket. I'd have to come in sometime tomorrow and finish the books. It would be easier to hire someone, but I didn't trust anyone to handle my finances. That was something my father taught me. I hated to admit it, but he was right.

I left the office and came face-to-face with Isabella. Thin, with a slender neck and a petite waistline, she looked like she was wasting away. She had lost more weight than she could afford, but her hair was just as silky and her features just as beautiful. The only reason she would be back here was if she was heading to my office. "Good evening, Isabella." I locked the door behind me so she wouldn't be tempted to fuck up my office. Breakups always led to bitter people. We had ended our arrangement nearly six months ago, but she still hadn't gotten over it. When I compared my thoughts and feelings for Rome to how I acted toward Isabella, I wasn't sure how Isabella got so attached to me. I wasn't even that nice to her—not like I was to Rome.

"Good evening, Calloway." In a black cocktail dress that hugged her tits together and showed her cleavage line, she looked stunning. Every man in that club wanted to get her on her knees, her ass in the air.

But I couldn't care less. "Is there something I can help you with?"

"Still seeing that little whore?"

My eyes narrowed in offense, and I had the urge to grab her by the throat—but not because I was aroused. "Talk about her like that again, and I'll ban you from Ruin. You're lucky I haven't done it already."

She pouted her lips in mock apology. "I thought being a whore was a good thing?"

It was hard to believe I ever cared about Isabella. Now, she just annoyed the shit out of me. "What do you want, Isabella? I'm very busy."

"Just wanted to see if you're still happy being her *boyfriend*." She emphasized the final word like it was an insult. "Wanted to check to see if you were tired of the same flavor every single night—vanilla."

She could only know those things if Jackson had told her. I'd have to kick his ass later. "Actually, the flavor has grown on me." I walked around her, making sure not to even brush my shoulder against hers. Her obsession with me wasn't the least bit attractive. Not like when I caught Rome staring at me. That lust in her eyes made me feel like a bigger man that I was.

Isabella's voice followed me as I walked away. "You can't keep up this charade much longer. Your dominance is going to get the best of you—and I'll be right here waiting."

I froze in the hallway, unsure why my feet stopped moving.

"I'll be ready to listen to your every command, to do everything you ask without question. I'll get on my knees simply because you say so. I'll submit—just the way you like."

I clenched both of my hands in desperation, wanting to do those exact things with Rome. I was attracted to her strong independence, but I also wanted that powerful woman to bow to me, to give me more control than I had ever had before. Some days, I thought I could live without that dominance. But moments like now made me realize just how impossible that was. It was something I needed in order to survive.

Would Rome ever give me that?

My feet began to move again, and I walked away without looking back, thinking about the woman I'd become blindly obsessed with. Rome trusted me in a way she never had before, and that made me feel guilty for not telling her the truth.

But I would come clean about everything.

When the time was right. I had to make sure her answer would be yes and that she wouldn't walk away from me. I knew I couldn't handle the loss. I knew I couldn't let her walk away.

Because she was my whole world.

I took Rome out to dinner before we headed back to my place. Christopher was enjoying his threesome, but I was enjoying myself more with his sister. Across the table, I enjoyed the tiny bites she took of her food. She still didn't eat much, but I'd gotten used to it. I never bothered with appetizers because that was an entire meal to her.

We returned to my place, and Isabella popped into my head. I thought about her offer to allow me to be her Dom whenever my relationship with Rome went south. Her obsession with me was inexplicable, but a part of me was intrigued by the offer. I didn't want any other woman but Rome, but I missed being a Dom. I missed being in control. I missed having my commands obeyed without resistance. Sexually, Rome usually complied with my demands. But outside of the bedroom, I could never get her to listen to me. That was an uphill battle —one I would never win.

"Everything alright?" She ran her hand across my back, soothing me.

I returned to the conversation, realizing my thoughts had drifted away. "Yeah...just trying to remember if I left a tip."

"Nope. But that's because I did." She grabbed the front of my jacket and pushed it off my shoulders until it hit the ground. Playfulness burned in her eyes as she gripped my tie and undid the knot with just a few fingers. Everything she did was sexy, and the fact that she wasn't even trying to be sexy just made her sexier. When the tie was separated, she grabbed both pieces and yanked me toward her.

I liked it—a lot.

But I also hated it. I hated letting someone else be in control, even for a second. It made me feel castrated and useless. It made me feel like less of a man, like I didn't deserve the woman I was with.

I yanked the tie from around my neck and wrapped it around hers instead. With a firm grip, I pulled her face to mine and kissed her hard on the mouth, taking back the control and feeling innately good about it. Her neck needed to be in my grasp. Her freedom needed to be mine as well.

Rome must not have cared about the change in roles because she kissed me back harder, panting into my mouth with arousal.

I lifted her into my chest and carried her upstairs into my bedroom, kissing her all the while. When I got her on my bed, I pinned her hands to the headboard and tied them to one of the wooden bars. When I bought this bed frame, my designer said she didn't like the look of it. The colors and finish didn't match my personality. But she didn't understand the kind of shit I did with the headboard.

Rome tugged on the tie, testing its strength. She could barely move because my knot was an expert one. She still had her dress and heels on, but I didn't need to get those off anyway. The only article of clothing that truly needed to be on the floor were her panties.

I undressed in front of her, slowly dropping everything with a thud on the rug. I kicked my shoes and yanked off my socks, keeping my eyes trained on her the entire time. I watched her lips part with a deep breath, her tongue peeking out slightly. When my cock came into view, she bit her bottom lip.

She was better than any submissive I'd ever had.

I crawled up the bed and started slow, kissing the inside of her knees and moving up slowly. Her black dress was still on, so my hands shoved her knees to her waist. My lips migrated, the scruff from my chin rubbing against the delicate area.

She yanked on the tie automatically, wanting to dig her fingers into my hair.

I pressed warm kisses against her cotton panties, moving over the fabric covering her throbbing clit. I deepened the kisses, soaking her underwear with my saliva as well as her own lubrication. Her legs widened and tensed as she rolled her head back, enjoying every second of what I was doing to her. A moan escaped her lips, a hint of my name on her tongue.

I'd had enough of the foreplay. This woman wanted me all the time, so it wasn't necessary. I just did it to tease her—and to tease myself.

I pulled her panties off and tossed them on top of my boxers. Then I moved between her legs, my cock rubbing against her slick pussy. I wanted to turn her over and smack her ass until it was red. My palm ached when I resisted the urge.

I positioned my face over hers, seeing her lips part in desperation for a kiss. Her elbows were next to her temples, and her nipples pointed toward the ceiling. I widened her legs with my arms, pinning her knees against her ribs. I wanted to fuck her hard, to take her like the prisoner she was. I wanted to give her so much of my cock she winced in pain. I wanted to make her cry from both pain and pleasure. And most of all, I wanted to hurt her.

But I wouldn't—for now.

I pressed my face close to hers but didn't kiss her, wanting to tease her as long as possible. My cock rubbed against her wet entrance, my length coated in her lubrication. I never had trouble getting a woman wet, but I'd never made a woman as wet as Rome. "You want me to fuck you, Vanilla?"

"Yes." She pulled on the tie, her hands going nowhere.

I kissed the corner of her mouth, pressing my steel length against her clit. I applied pressure and ground against her throbbing nub, making her move her hips back into me, moaning at the same time.

"Fuck me, Calloway," she whispered. "Please."

Fuck. Nothing hotter than a beautiful woman begging to be fucked.

"You want me to fuck you hard, Vanilla?"

"So hard that you can't call me Vanilla anymore."

The hair on the back of my neck stood on end, and my cock twitched in response. She said a lot of sexy things, but that had to be a top pick for me. Sometimes she walked in the shadows with me, being one with the darkness. It made me feel less alone, like I could have everything I wanted with this innocent woman.

I meant to tease her, but she somehow teased me. I slipped my cock inside her, pushing through her tight wetness until I was completely buried. I was balls deep, implanted deep in her channel where no man had ever gone before.

I looked down at her, seeing her hard nipples and red chest, her beautiful brown hair cascading across the pillow, and my cock buried deep inside her pussy. Her hands were pinned above her head, her fair skin flawless.

I wanted this moment to last forever.

The second I started to move inside her, I wanted to come. I wanted to pound as much come inside her as possible, filling her to the brim like every other night. But something felt different tonight.

My fingers dug into the muscles of her thighs, and I listened to her deep breathing. Her tits moved toward the sky with every breath, her nipples begging to be pinched between my forefinger and thumb. Missionary was my least favorite position, but she made it the most erotic experience of my life.

I slid through her wet channel, feeling her intimately. My cock was in heaven and never wanted to leave, welcomed by her warmth. I'd never gotten so much pleasure from fucking other women. I didn't know if it was because Rome was a virgin, because she was exceptionally beautiful, or because she could slap like a boss. But whatever it was, it got my engine going.

My hips rocked gently into her, but then they developed a mind of their own. They began to thrust hard, fucking her with speed and agility. The headboard tapped against the wall rhythmically.

"Harder."

I moaned and worked my body to give her what she wanted, fucking her with as much strength as I could. My headboard began to crash into the wall, leaving dents and marks.

Like I gave a fuck.

Rome moaned incoherently, her words muffled by her screams. When she came, she tightened around me and yanked so hard on the silk tie that she nearly ripped it. A few seams broke, but it remained intact. Her head rolled back, and she screamed like a dying animal, my name muffled by the sounds she made. "Oh god..." She closed her eyes as she enjoyed the remaining high that was slowly depleting from her body. Her pussy gradually released my cock, allowing it to slide through with less resistance.

"You put on quite a show, sweetheart." I leaned over her and kissed her on the mouth, tasting the salt from her sweat. I pumped into her a few more times, preparing for the grand finale. I loved the beginning, the middle, and the end. But coming inside her was a supernatural experience. I touched heaven and hell at the exact same time.

I released inside her, getting lost in the overwhelming pleasure this woman gave me. I'd come inside her more times than I could count, and each experience was better than the last. I sucked her nipple into my mouth and tasted her flesh as I finished. "I want to keep you tied up like that forever." I wanted to keep her as a prisoner, her sole purpose to please me around the clock, ensuring she had no other life outside these walls. I would be the center of her universe.

"Then you should." The fire was back in her eyes already, wanting another round even though mounds of my come were already sitting inside her.

I pulled her bottom lip into my mouth and nicked her with my teeth, applying strong pressure without breaking the skin. "Maybe I will."

We lay in bed together, both satisfied from our evening of fucking. I didn't feel guilty for not getting any work done today for Ruin because spending time with Rome was a much better utilization of my time.

She traced her fingers down my chest, feeling the grooves of my abs. "How's your brother?"

I didn't like talking about other men when we were in bed together. I would've commanded her to never say such a thing again if she were my submissive. I clenched my jaw and waited for the anger to pass, knowing I had no right to tell her off. Isabella was right when she said I wouldn't be able to do this forever. Already, I felt myself beginning to crack. The more time I spent with Rome, the more possessive I became. And the more possessive I became, the more controlling I wanted to be. "I'm sure he's good. Haven't seen him much lately."

"It's interesting. Even when I wasn't living with Christopher, I would still talk to him a few times a week."

"That's because Christopher isn't an asshole."

She chuckled. "You obviously don't know him very well."

Actually, she didn't know *me* very well. "Jackson and I have never been close. He's always resented me because he assumed our father favored me."

"Why did he assume that?" She continued to touch me, stroking her fingers across my chiseled physique.

"My father left most of his inheritance to me. Jackson didn't get anything." When I read his will, I could hardly believe it. The man spent most of his life hating me, chasing me down the hallway with a bat. It wasn't until I became a man that I started fighting back. That only pushed him harder because he no longer had the control. But I met his ferocity with my own. It wasn't until years after his death that I realized what our problem was.

We were too much alike.

The first time I tied up a woman and whipped her, I came so hard I screamed. In that moment, I knew I was just as sick as he was. I knew growing up in his shadow had made me just like him. And I suspected he'd realized it too.

"Why is that?" she whispered. Her head lay on the pillow beside me, her beautiful eyes gleaming in the dark.

"Not sure. Sometimes I wonder if it was his form of an apology." My father and I only talked about business. We hardly ever talked about Mom. When she was admitted to a facility, he never mentioned her again. It was like she'd never existed to begin with. He was the coldest man I've ever known—and I knew I'd inherited that same trait.

"Maybe," she said. "But money can't make things right."

She was right about that. The money had never changed my opinion of him. If he knew I used most of it to start up Humanitarians United, he'd be convulsing in his grave right now. "No, it can't. Jackson has always been jealous that he got cut out of the will. That's why we disagree so much."

"Does he know?"

I knew what she was asking. "No. I never told him."

"Why?"

I'd been through a lot of pain, but I'd never suffered as much as I did when someone I loved struggled. Seeing my mom lose her mind was much worse than a knife to the stomach. Seeing her stare at me without an ounce of recognition was worse than a bullet to the head. "I don't want Jackson to feel guilty."

"Why would he feel guilty?"

"Because I took all the beatings so he didn't have to. When Jackson did something wrong, I always took the blame. He never knew about any of that…"

Rome looked at me with affection, her hand grazing over my heart. "You're so sweet, Calloway."

Sometimes. But most of the time, I was just evil.

"I understand how you feel. I would never want Christopher to be in any pain. I love him too much."

I wouldn't say I loved my brother…but he was still family.

"You should tell him, Calloway."

"No." I preferred the distance between us rather than a new bond through suffering.

"If he knew the truth, maybe things would be different."

"Maybe. But would that really make anything better?"

She leaned into me and pressed a kiss to the skin over my heart, her lips soft and warm. "You never know. At least it would help him understand what happened. Help him understand his older brother better."

I watched her kiss me, moved by the slight affection. I'd never let a woman be so gentle with me. I preferred being slapped in the face to a kiss on the shoulder. But Rome made me feel so good that I couldn't stop her.

I never wanted to stop her.

When it came to Rome, I felt like two different men. I felt like a man in a romance novel, someone who cared about a woman he couldn't live without. But I also felt like a demon who moaned at the thought of hurting something so delicate. I was never both men at one time —only one or the other.

———

I sat at my desk and stared at my computer screen. I

had just received an email from a donor asking about our annual blood drive, but the words blurred together, and I couldn't decipher them.

I couldn't pay attention because of Rome.

She was just down the hall, thirty yards away on the other side of the building. I knew she wore that green dress I liked because she got ready at my place that morning. She wore a gold necklace that hung low and matched her earrings. Her hair was pulled back so every exquisite feature could be seen. She was so beautiful, it hurt. A part of me couldn't blame Dean for making a move.

But I still wanted to rip out his throat anyway.

I couldn't explain the feeling that came over me. Just an hour ago, I was fine. I arranged a lunch meeting with my secretary, and then I examined the revised budget reports that Dean had sent over.

But now I felt hollow.

All I wanted was Rome, to feel her in my arms and smell her hair. I wanted to touch that heavenly soft skin and feel the goose bumps form on her arms as I touched her. My mouth craved her lips, the taste of vanilla from her ChapStick teasing my senses.

The feeling wasn't sexual in the least. It was something else entirely.

I hit the intercom and spoke directly to my assistant.

"Please ask Ms. Moretti to step into my office for a moment."

"Right away, sir."

I leaned back in the chair and waited for the large black doors to open. My office had the most privacy of any other room in the building. I kept it that way on purpose, wanting my authority to be mysterious. People never became too friendly with me, always keeping their distance.

The less people knew about me, the better.

The door opened, and Rome walked inside, closing it behind her and looking just as beautiful as she had that morning. Her sleek ponytail highlighted the natural curves of her face. If she'd lived in a different era of history, civilizations would worship her as a goddess. She stopped in front of my desk, her hands together at her waist. "Did you need something, Mr. Owens?"

I didn't like it when she addressed me that way. Calloway or Sexy was much better. "Yes." I walked around the desk until I was right in front of her, just a few feet away.

Her cheeks flushed slightly, and her breathing elevated, suspecting the close proximity wasn't going to be professional. She did her eye makeup differently this morning, making them stand out in a breathtaking way.

I took a step forward so we were close together. My

eyes went to her lips, seeing the way they slightly broke apart as if she expected a kiss. My hands went to her petite waist, and I gripped her firmly, making sure she couldn't slip away. I pressed my forehead to hers and closed my eyes, enjoying the overwhelming power that surged within me.

"Calloway...we can't do this."

"Ten minutes," I whispered. "I'm not going to kiss you. I'm not going to fuck you. I just want to hold you." My hand snaked to the back of her neck where I could feel her gentle pulse. The smell of roses washed over me, and I inhaled deeply, feeling the sting of the breath. There was something about the way she made me feel... it was addictive. It felt like a form of happiness, an indescribable joy. I didn't know what this woman was doing to me. I wasn't even sure if it was good or bad.

"Everything okay?"

"Yes." I pressed a kiss to her forehead before I returned my head against hers. My hands moved to her shoulders and down her arms, feeling the smooth skin and the goose bumps I'd expected to feel. Her reaction to me was just as powerful as mine was to her. "I missed you. I tried writing an email, but I couldn't stop thinking about you." I'd spent all night with her, her hands bound to my headboard, but it just wasn't enough.

"I always miss you…"

I pulled her closer into my chest and rested her cheek over my heart. Her tits were firm against me, but the touch didn't get me hard. My need for her wasn't sexual — and that was the most surprising thing of all.

When ten minutes had passed, I knew I needed to let her go. "I'll let you get back to work…"

She reluctantly pulled away, her stance on our office romance unclear. When it came to affection at Humanitarians United, she wanted nothing to do with it. She didn't want a single person in the building to know we slept in the same bed. But now, her position had weakened. She looked at me with desire in her eyes, wanting our embrace to never end. "You want to get dinner tonight?"

I didn't need to give her my answer. "I'll pick you up at six."

9

ROME

"Christopher, I need help." I was flustered the second I walked in the door.

"What's up?" He stood at the kitchen counter, talking with his mouth full. He made half a sandwich but couldn't stop eating it for one second so he could talk to me. He leaned against the counter and crossed his ankles, still in his suit.

I set my bag on the entryway table and slipped off my heels from hell. Throughout the workday, they weren't so bad. But by the time I walked home, I was dying. I was in so much pain I wanted to take them off and walk barefoot on the defiled sidewalk of New York City. "It's about Calloway."

"What about him?" He took another bite, chewing loudly.

"Could you stop eating for just a second?"

"Could you wait to dump your boyfriend problems on me until I'm finished?" he countered, a smartass look on his face.

I ignored his final comment and powered through. "I've been seeing Calloway for six months, and I know that's not that long, but I think I might..." I couldn't believe I was about to say this out loud. Once I did, it would really be true. "I think I love him."

Christopher looked just as bored as he had a minute ago. "And your point?"

"I'm not sure if I should tell him. We haven't been seeing each other very long."

"Six months?" he asked incredulously. "That's like an eternity. No guy sticks with a woman that long unless it's going somewhere."

"I guess you're right. But I'm not sure how he'll react."

Christopher finally finished his sandwich and wiped the crumbs off his fingers. "If he's stuck it out with you this long, I doubt anything bad could come from it. He's hung up on you, so there's a good chance he feels the same way."

"You think so?"

"Yeah. And even if he doesn't, he probably wouldn't be weirded out by it. Now, if some girl said that to me, I'd be out of there faster than the speed of light."

I didn't see too many similarities between Christopher and Calloway, so that was good news.

"Just go with your instinct. If you love the guy, tell him. What harm could it do?"

Probably none.

"Can we wrap up the girl talk?" he asked. "I have a date with this copy editor for the *Times*. She asked me out at lunch."

"Cool. What's she like?"

He shrugged. "Hot."

"And that's it?"

"Yep."

"Didn't you just eat?" I asked. "Now you're going to dinner?"

"I said we're going on a date. I didn't say anything about dinner."

"Then what are you going to do on this date?"

"Fuck." He walked out of the kitchen and headed down the hallway into his bedroom.

I forgot about Christopher and sat on the couch, thinking about my morning in Calloway's office. He held me for several minutes for no reason at all. He ran his fingers through my hair and touched me so softly. I felt like a diamond, a prized jewel he cherished.

I felt like the most important thing in the world.

After everything I'd been through, I didn't think I

could trust someone the way I trusted him. I didn't think I could find someone who made my heart race like this. He was everything I wanted in a partner, and I actually believed I was getting my chance for a normal life. I'd always hoped I'd meet a man as perfect as Calloway. And now that I actually had, it made my horrific past seem insignificant.

I knew how I felt. Actually, I'd known for a while. But when he touched me like that, held me like I was the most special thing in the world, I wondered if he felt the same way. He was different from how he was in the beginning. He didn't open up to me about the man he truly was. But he'd opened up about his past, his nightmares, and his complicated relationship with his brother. Instead of feeling like a couple, I felt like a team.

My phone vibrated with a message, and I wasn't surprised to see his name on the screen. *I know I said 6. But I'm coming to get you now. Hope you're ready.*

As always, his message made me smile. *I'm always ready for you.*

After dinner, we relaxed on the couch in front of the TV. I was still in my dress, and my heels sat in a pile on the floor. I lay on his chest, feeling it rise and fall with his deep breathing. Even though I felt his hard-on underneath me, he didn't make a move for sex.

His hand moved up and down my back, sliding into the steep curve above my ass before he moved back up again. Normally, he tried to get me naked right after dinner, but tonight, he didn't seem interested. "Are you doing anything on Saturday?"

"No plans yet."

"There's somewhere I'd like to take you."

"It sounds like a surprise." I sat up and looked down into his face, my hair forming a curtain over his left cheek.

"Something like that." He sat up, moving me with him effortlessly. He kept going until my back was against the couch. His cock was hard through his jeans, and he ground against my panties as he held himself over me. He kissed my neck as he grabbed my panties and pulled them down my long legs.

My body clenched in excitement, eager to have him deep inside me. It didn't matter how many times we'd made love, I always wanted more. I never knew sex could be this fantastic. It was stupid for me to have waited so long.

Calloway moved his mouth to mine and kissed me slowly as his fingers slipped between my legs and played with me. He rubbed my clit with gentle pressure and then inserted his fingers inside me, feeling my sticky lubrication. "Always so wet…"

"For you."

He growled against my mouth and continued to tease me, his fingers moving farther inside me until he had me panting underneath him. "Sweetheart, I want to try something different tonight, and I know you're brave enough to do it."

If he wanted to tie me up again, I had no complaints. Being taken over and over throughout the night was a fantasy come true. "And what would that be?"

He pulled his fingers out then shoved his cock inside me, my lubrication coating every inch of him as he slipped inside. He closed his eyes and moaned quietly as he entered, stretching out my tight pussy for the hundredth time. "Do you trust me, sweetheart?" He pressed his mouth against mine as he spoke, his lips brushing against mine as they moved.

There wasn't a doubt in my mind. "Yes."

His eyes darkened in satisfaction, and he thrust inside me, taking me gently, unlike the other night. He dug his hand into my hair as he kissed me, his chest pressed against mine. We breathed together, our legs tangled. Every thrust felt better than the last, and I found myself wanting to stay like this for the rest of time.

His hand trailed down my body until he moved between my legs. His fingers brushed against my thigh before he turned me to the side. He lay beside me on the couch, his back to the cushion. Our lovemaking didn't stop with our movements, and Calloway had the skill to keep the fire going.

His hand grazed past the back of my leg until his fingers moved into the crack between my cheeks. The second I felt him, I knew what was going to happen, but I didn't push his hand away. The last time his fingers were there, the sensation felt foreign and unwelcome. But as he continued to move inside me and kiss me, it felt natural. When I came, it was harder than I ever had before.

So I guess I liked it.

His fingers were still wet from my pussy, so he inserted them into my back entrance, sliding in with less resistance than last time.

Calloway opened his eyes and rubbed his nose against mine. "If you want me to stop, all you have to do is say so." He kissed the corner of my mouth before the passion returned, my mouth feeling numb and hot at the same time.

I explored with my hands, touching every inch that

I'd already touched before. He was six foot three of pure man, but the package he wore was nothing compared to the man underneath. He was compassionate, gentle, and powerful.

I was just about to come when he pulled his length out of me.

I wanted to scream at the loss.

He looked into my eyes as he adjusted my leg, practically pinning my knee to my chest. He took control, doing whatever he wanted to my body like he owned it. His hand wrapped around the base of his cock, and he pressed the head into my ass.

Something I hadn't been expecting.

His arm was tucked in the crook of my neck, supporting my head as he slid inside me. "Touch yourself, sweetheart."

I hadn't touched myself in so long I nearly forgot how.

He sucked my bottom lip and released a moan. "Now."

I responded to his command instantly, my fingers moving to my throbbing nub. The second I touched myself, I felt the electricity. I forgot about the enormous cock penetrating me from the backside.

He continued to slide inside me, watching my reaction as his impressive dick stretched my ass wider than it ever had. "It'll hurt at first. But it'll get better." He kissed me and moved his dick almost entirely within me, pushing me to the limit.

I moaned as he slid out only to slide in again. It hurt me more than it pleased me, but the pleasure on his face made me allow it. Anytime his dick was inside me, hard for me, I felt special. So I kept an open mind and let him continue, hoping it would get better as we moved along.

"Touch yourself harder, sweetheart." He grabbed my wrist and made the motion for me, not directly touching me with the fingers that had already explored me. He used my knuckles to change the movements of my fingers, and I couldn't believe a man knew how to touch a woman better than I did.

When I finally felt the pleasure everywhere, I ignored the pain. His massive cock didn't feel so excruciating. The more I relaxed, the easier it was to accommodate him. The building orgasm that I felt earlier had returned, slowly approaching with a fiery crash.

"Together," he commanded.

Even without being inside me, he knew when I was going to explode. I gripped his arm as an anchor, feeling his cock ram into me harder. I felt the climax build until it could no longer be contained. Heat surged through my body just before it hit at full speed. "Oh god…"

He gripped my hip as he pounded his cock into me, being aggressive as he pushed his seed farther and farther inside me.

The effect of all the sensations gave me a better orgasm than I'd ever had before. Being full of him in a new way heightened my experience, making me feel something so unique and oddly wonderful. The orgasm seemed to last forever, nearly an eternity.

When Calloway finished, he remained buried in my ass. Slowly, he softened, his cock gently sliding out of me. He pressed his forehead to mine, his eyes on my lips. "Thank you for trusting me."

I was exhausted from the euphoria that had just swept through my body. I watched his lips move but didn't gather any meaning from them. My head rested on the pillow, and I closed my eyes, aware of his cock still inside me.

Calloway grabbed the blanket hanging over the back of the couch and pulled it on top of both of us. He settled beside me, sharing the same pillow. "I don't think I can call you Vanilla anymore."

"I still like sweetheart."

He chuckled. "Sweetheart, it is."

Cynthia, Calloway's assistant, called my office phone. "Mr. Owens would like to see you in his office. He wants you to bring the schedule for this month."

I knew that was bogus. He didn't give a damn about the schedule. "I'll be there in two seconds."

"Alright."

I grabbed my folder and walked down the hallway to his office, sometimes wondering if people noticed I went to Calloway's office more often that I should. I was the new girl, so hopefully, they assumed I needed extra help with my projects.

I definitely didn't want to be known as the office whore.

Cynthia nodded for me to go inside, so I walked in, making sure to close the door behind me.

He was leaning against his desk like usual, looking like a president with the skyscrapers of the city in the background. With his arms crossed over his chest, Calloway's shoulders looked broad and powerful. He hadn't shaved in two days, so the hair around his face was thicker than usual. Hair or no hair, he looked equally sexy—in my opinion.

"I take it you didn't call me in here to really talk about the schedule?" I held up the folder.

The only answer I got was a slight head shake.

I set the folder on the chair and crossed my arms over my chest, playing his game. "Then why am I in here?" We were so supposed to be professional in the workplace, but we've already had two slipups. Sometimes I wondered if it would be easier just to be honest with everyone.

He walked toward me and inserted his hands in his pockets. "I wanted to know how you were doing."

"How I'm doing?" I asked in surprise. "The same as I was this morning."

"I didn't get to see you this morning. I left for the gym." He was one of those fit people who woke up at five in the morning just to work out. Absolutely insane, but whatever.

"Well, you could have asked me that after work. Or even texted me."

"I wanted to look at you." His hands slid around my waist then gripped my ass. "And to see if you were sore today."

I hadn't experienced any discomfort, remarkably. And honestly, I'd been so busy at work I hadn't thought about it much. "No. I'm fine."

The corner of his mouth rose in a smile. "You're tougher than I give you credit for."

"Maybe I enjoyed it so much last night it didn't hurt."

His smile dropped, and his eyes darkened. "Yeah?"

I nodded.

"I'm glad you kept an open mind."

"I don't have an open mind." If any other guy tried that stunt with me, I wouldn't have allowed it. But Calloway was different. He'd been my one and only exception. The first time I laid eyes on him, I had no idea how he was going to change my life—in only good ways. "I just trust you."

The darkness left his gaze, replaced by a calm softness. "You have no idea how much that means to me." His hand moved to the steep curve in my back, and he placed a small kiss in the corner of my mouth. It was PG, tame enough that we could both pull away without ripping each other's clothes off. "I'll let you get back to work."

"I'll see you later." I turned around and bent over to grab the folder.

He smacked my ass playfully. "Later, baby."

10

CALLOWAY

We woke up on Saturday morning, the sheets tucked around us as we lay in a tangle of arms and legs. Her scent was permanently infused in my sheets, and the smell was intoxicating. Her presence left a mark on all of my household things, but now I liked the change. Once upon a time, it was impossible for me to share my personal space. Isabella hadn't been to my home once.

I woke up first, so I watched Rome sleep beside me, noticing the way her mouth opened slightly when she breathed. Her teeth were cute, and her soft lips were always wonderful to the touch. Even though my t-shirts were baggy on her, she rocked them like a supermodel.

Subconsciously, she must have known I was staring at her because she suddenly stirred and opened her eyes. Heavy and full of sleep, they fought to stay open.

But once she took in my face, a beautiful smile stretched over her lips. "Hey, Sexy..." Her palm immediately brushed over my cheek, feeling the beard that was coming in. I hadn't shaved in a few days, and I couldn't tell which she preferred.

"Hey, sweetheart." My hand moved over her flat stomach, knowing my come was still sitting inside her from the night before. "Sleep well?"

She stretched her arms over her head. "I always sleep well over here. This bed is amazing, and the teddy bear that comes with it is perfect."

"Teddy bear, huh? I think I'm more manly than a stuffed animal."

"But just as cute." She chuckled then tapped her finger against my nose like I was a child.

I chuckled then pulled her to my chest, my lips moving over her temple and kissing her as I went. "Let's get some breakfast. There's somewhere I want to take you this afternoon."

"That's right," she said. "The surprise."

"It's not really a surprise in the way you're thinking. Just something I want you to see." I kissed her neck before I left the bed and pulled on my boxers and sweatpants. When I turned around, her eyes were glued to my backside. "See something you like?"

"You have the nicest ass," she said. "It's not something I ever paid attention to before. But then again, I've never met another guy with a tight ass like that."

I smiled. "If you think my ass is nice, you should see yours." I gave her a gentle smack on the behind. "How do pancakes sound?"

"Ooh...and bacon. I'm in the mood for greasy, crunchy bacon."

She hardly ever had an appetite, so I knew she was in a good mood. "And some eggs. Need some lean protein."

She rolled her eyes. "I'm not in the mood to be healthy."

"Well, if you want my ass to stay tight, I need to watch what I eat."

She crawled out of bed. "I don't care about having a tight ass, so bring on the bacon."

Hand in hand, we walked into the assisted-living facility.

"What are we doing here?" Rome asked.

"There's this woman I read to."

"Aww...that's sweet."

I approached the nurse's station in the lobby and saw Diane.

Her smile lit up the entire room when she looked at me. "Calloway, it's always so nice to see you."

"Thanks, Diane. How is she today?"

The woman beckoned us to follow her down the hall until we arrived at my mother's room. As usual, she was sitting outside on the balcony, looking at the deep green grass of the lawn, beside an arrangement of colored flowers.

"She's pretty good." Diane waited by the door. "Just had breakfast, so she's less grouchy." She winked then walked out.

"What's her name?" Rome whispered as we walked to the balcony.

"Theresa." The patio door was opened, so I stepped on through, a Harry Potter book tucked under my arm. Anytime a normal son saw his mother, he probably greeted her with a hug. But I hadn't hugged my mom in nearly a decade.

She sat in the rocking chair, her knitting on her lap. Her dark hair was curled in a classy way, her champagne pink top going well with her skin tone. Even if she didn't remember who she was or where she lived, she still groomed herself every morning.

When she noticed me, she looked up. "Hello. How are you?"

I extended my hand to shake hers, for the umpteenth time. "Calloway Owens. I'm from Humanitarians United. I've come to read to you today."

She eyed my hand almost suspiciously before she took it. "Oh, that's nice. I have so much knitting to do I never have time to read."

I smiled before I introduced Rome. "And this is... my girlfriend. Her name is Rome, and she also works with me." If my mother could remember anything, she would be so happy to see me with a woman. She'd always nagged me to settle down, even before I turned eighteen. What she'd wanted more than anything else in the world was grandchildren.

"Oh, that's lovely." Mom smiled before she shook Rome's hand. "You're a beautiful girl. Good. Calloway is a very handsome man, so you two go well together."

Rome chuckled. "That's nice of you to say."

I pulled out a chair for Rome so she could sit down. Then I sat beside her.

My mom watched me with astute eyes, blue and clear like my own. Sometimes I wondered if she recognized me, or at least felt a sense of familiarity. But she never connected the dots, never remembered her oldest son. "Calloway...that's a nice name. I like it."

I nodded. "Thank you."

"Your mother has good taste."

"She certainly does." I held up the Harry Potter book. "Would you like me to begin reading?"

"Sure." She turned back to her knitting, her short brown hair falling forward as she looked down. She was just as thin as ever, never having an appetite, even when she was well. But she still held herself like a queen. My mother was beautiful despite her age, and I saw so much of myself when I looked into her face. Sometimes I saw Jackson too.

"Would you like to read?" I handed the book off to Rome.

"Sure." Rome opened the book to the first page. "I'm not a performer, but I'll do my best."

"I'm sure it'll be lovely, dear," Mom said, using the yarn in her lap to knit a scarf.

I'd read the beginning of that Harry Potter book at least a hundred times. I practically had it memorized. Without the book in front of me, I could quote every line and every event.

Rome began to read, her beautiful voice soothing and enjoyable.

We spent the afternoon there, and Rome read so long she nearly finished the book. My mother listened, rocking the chair as she continued to focus on the work her hands were doing. Eventually, Rome grew tired and placed a bookmark between the pages. "I'm gonna lose my voice pretty soon…"

I rested my hand on her thigh. "We should get going anyway." I rose to my feet and approached my mom, feeling the same pain I felt every time I had to leave. It would be easier not to bother coming at all, to give up hope that maybe one day her memory would come back to her. But I couldn't live with that kind of guilt. If the situation were reversed, I knew my mom would always be by my side—no matter what. I wouldn't feel like a man if I didn't give her the same loyalty. Jackson claimed visiting her was pointless—and stupid. But I suspected he couldn't handle the sight of her demise. He'd always been more sensitive than I was—even if he wouldn't admit it. "We'll see you again next week, Theresa." I grabbed her hand and gave it a squeeze.

My mom smiled up at me and rested her other hand on top of mine. "You're such a wonderful man, Calloway."

My heart nearly burst at the unexpected affection.

"I know it isn't much, and I'm sure you don't wear this sort of thing, but…" She held up the finished scarf and placed it into my hand. "It's all I have to give. I'd like you to have it."

I felt the soft fabric in my fingertips, and instantly, tears burned behind my eyes. I hadn't felt emotion like this since I was a child, an undeniable sensation deep in my gut. I hadn't felt anything besides permanent numbness. "Thank you…" I hooked the black and blue scarf around my neck, not caring what anyone thought of me.

She smiled then shook Rome's hand. "You give him beautiful children someday, alright?"

Rome chuckled. "I'll try. It was so nice to meet you, Theresa." Rome kissed her on the cheek then walked to the door.

I stayed in front of my mother, wanting to say more than just a generic goodbye. I wanted to thank her for all she had done for me when I was growing up. I never had the opportunity to show her the gratitude she deserved, for taking care of my laundry every day and putting food on the table. They were all little things, but they added up in time. Jackson and I were her entire life until she lost her mind. Coming here every week to read to her didn't begin to repay everything she had done for me. "I'll see you soon."

I walked out with Rome and grabbed her hand, wanting the affection that would keep me stable.

Emotion never came easy for me, but whenever I visited this facility, I walked out a little weaker than when I walked inside.

"She's sweet," Rome said. "How long have you been doing this?"

"About seven years."

"You've been reading to the same woman for seven years?" she asked incredulously, eyeing me with surprise as we headed to the parking lot where the car was parked.

"Yeah."

"And she doesn't remember you?"

"Her mind resets every morning when she wakes up." She didn't remember my father or her two children. She didn't remember where she was born. Her entire life never happened because she couldn't remember it.

"Poor thing," she whispered. "She's lucky to have you, Calloway."

I reached the car and opened the passenger door. "I'm her son. I'll always be there for her." I didn't make eye contact with Rome after I said the words, knowing what kind of reaction I would get from her.

Rome was about to enter the car but stopped when she heard what I said. Her gaze moved to my face, and all the joy she'd possessed that afternoon disappeared.

Sadness entered her expression, and her eyes immediately welled up with tears.

I finally looked at her directly, seeing my pain mirrored back at me. I had no idea why I'd brought Rome here today. I wasn't sure why I told her the truth about my mother. For some reason, I wanted to share it with her, not to carry the pain on my own.

"Calloway..." She moved into my chest and hugged me around the waist, her face buried into my t-shirt. "I'm so sorry."

I wrapped my arms around her shoulders, still wearing the scarf my mother knitted for me. "I know." I moved my lips to her forehead and pressed a gentle kiss against her warm skin. "I know, sweetheart."

Rome must have sensed I didn't feel like talking for the rest of the evening because she didn't say much. She sat with me on the couch, cuddled into my side with her head resting on my shoulder. She wore my sweatpants and t-shirt, looking sexy in the oversized clothes.

I watched TV but didn't really pay attention to what I was watching. My mind drifted in a quiet moment, thinking about everything that had happened today. I didn't know what possessed me to bring Rome to the assisted-living facility. There was no premeditated thought. I just decided to ask her—so I did it.

I was extremely quiet about my personal life. The only other person who knew about my mother was Jackson. And even then, I would have kept it a secret from him if I could. I pursued Rome because I wanted her to be my submissive, to obey all my commands without question. Yet, I did something I never would have done with any of my submissives.

What was wrong with me?

Rome moved up my chest and straddled my hips with her long legs. Her pussy was right over my cock, and within seconds, I would be hard, like always. She placed both of her palms against my chest and gently moved up and down, caressing me while looking into my eyes. There wasn't any sympathy in her gaze, but there wasn't a sexual appetite either. "Thank you for taking me with you today."

My hands moved to her thighs, and I caressed the powerful muscles through her sweatpants. Rome didn't hit the gym, but she walked everywhere she went. As a result, she was strong. I liked that about her.

"If you ever want to talk about it, you know I'm here."

I looked into her eyes, my mouth immobile. There was nothing to say about my mother. She was in that facility because she couldn't take care of herself. Obviously, I couldn't give her what she needed around the clock. Placing her in someone else's care was all I could do. "The doctors can't figure out what the problem is. She doesn't have Alzheimer's."

"Oh…"

"I think her mind snapped when she realized all the horrible things my father was doing. She couldn't handle it, so she checked out. But now that so many years have passed, I suspect something else happened in her mind, something that doctors can't figure out."

Rome rubbed my chest gently, the pity rising. "You're a good son, Calloway. Does Jackson visit her too?"

"Never. Says it's pointless."

She massaged my shoulders, her body weightless on top of mine. "I wish there was something I could do…"

"You're doing it, sweetheart." My hands circled her small waistline, feeling the muscles of her core.

Her hands wrapped around my wrists, and she gripped me gently, her hair falling over one shoulder. The brown strands were soft to the touch but strong. When I wrapped her hair around my fist, I could make her do my bidding.

She leaned forward and cupped my face, her beautiful eyes gazing at mine. Her features were more perfect than the stars in the nighttime sky, bright and beautiful. With or without makeup, she was gorgeous. And when she looked at me like that, like I was her whole world, I felt more like a man than ever before.

When I first saw her in that bar months ago, I'd never felt so much energy surge through my body. All I wanted to do was fuck her, but now, I respected her as a close friend. Sometimes I wanted to hold her just for the sake of it. With Isabella, there was no affection unless my cock was in her pussy, mouth, or ass.

Rome gave me a soft kiss on the mouth, her touch delicate and full of affection. When she pulled away, she had an emotional look in her eyes, feeling some kind of pain I couldn't see. "I love you, Calloway. I don't know when it happened, and I wasn't sure if I could ever feel this way for someone...but it did happen." She trailed her hands from my face back to my chest, looking at me with the same expression.

I heard what she said. It was crystal clear. But it was the last thing I expected her to say. We'd only been seeing each other for six months, and I'd told her I wasn't looking for marriage and a happily ever after.

This was something I'd never anticipated.

She said it with such heart, such affection, and I felt like an ass for not saying it back.

But I couldn't.

Love wasn't in my vocabulary. Love wasn't something I was capable of feeling. Affection and devotion were all I could offer her.

She continued to stare at me, waiting for me to say something.

I was surprised my reaction wasn't to push her off of me and run. I was surprised I didn't want to end our relationship then and there. Her words terrified me, but there was nothing she could say that would make me walk away. "Rome…"

Her eyes fell in sadness, catching my tone.

"A long time ago, I said I wasn't looking for marriage and forever… I meant that." I swallowed the lump in my throat, feeling like an asshole for rejecting her confession. She put her heart on the line and left herself vulnerable, but I couldn't give her what she wanted, even to spare her pain.

Her eyes moved down to my chest, where her hands still rested.

A beautiful day had been ruined, and I knew I wouldn't be able to fix it. If she walked away, I couldn't stop her. But I didn't want to give her up, so I hoped she would stay. I hoped she would give this a real chance because it had so much potential.

When she spoke, her voice was still strong. "It's

okay, Calloway." She looked at me again, determination in her eyes.

"What's okay?" Rome usually said exactly what she meant, but in this instance, I couldn't figure it out. It was okay that I didn't tell her I loved her? It was okay that I didn't want to spend the rest of my life with her?

"It's okay that you didn't say it back. Because I know how you really feel, Calloway. It was difficult for me to come to this realization too, to take down my walls long enough to actually let someone in. You need more time—and that's perfectly okay."

I stared at her in awe, surprised someone had the confidence to be rejected then hold her head high. She had misplaced faith in me after I hurt her. Despite everything I'd claimed, she still believed otherwise. She valued herself and noticed the way I treated her, assuming there was more underneath my cold exterior. "I appreciate how well you're taking this but—"

"I know what you're going to say, so you should just stop."

"And what am I going to say?"

"That you don't love me and never will. That you don't see a future for us. That it's just not in your nature. I'm sure you believe all of those things, but I know better. For the past six months we've been together, I've seen you change.

I've seen you open up and take me in little by little. I understand it's hard for you. Believe me, I do. But one day, you're going to finally admit to yourself how you feel about us—about me. You were patient with me when I asked you to be, and now I'll be patient with you. I don't need to hear you say you love me—because I know you do."

I couldn't take my eyes off her, mesmerized by this powerful woman. When she put her mind to something, she didn't change it. I could correct her as many times as I wanted, but it wouldn't make a difference. The honorable thing to do was to walk away from this relationship since I couldn't give her what she deserved. But I was too weak for that. Rome made me happy, and I wasn't ready to let her go. I wasn't ready to walk away from the sexiest woman I'd ever laid eyes on. I was a selfish man, and I couldn't stop myself from being selfish.

She grabbed her shirt and pulled it over her head, revealing her perfect tits for me to enjoy. "Now, make love to me." She stared me down with green fire in her eyes, looking unbelievably sexy. Her confidence turned me on more than her submissiveness. It was a paradox I couldn't explain. I didn't bother to contradict her and tell her that I didn't make love to anyone. Instead, I grabbed her by her tiny waist and threw her on the couch, my cock harder than ever before. I wanted to be deep inside her, to take everything she was giving me. I wanted to give her so much of my come she couldn't handle it.

And I wanted to do that for the rest of the night.

I sat at my desk in the office at Ruin. The bass from the music echoed down the hallway and reached my ears if I concentrated hard enough. The rhythmic beat was constant, shaking the foundation as well as the walls of this place.

This club once belonged to my father, but he used it in more sinister ways. Looking to make a quick buck from abducting young women naïve enough to enter a place like this out of curiosity, he sold some of them into sex trafficking. Others were made into his own prisoners. I grew up watching him whip women until they convulsed on the floor.

I promised myself I would never be so cruel, that I would lead a different life from my father. I upheld that promise—but not entirely. I'd inherited his need for pain, to hurt women to get off. I enjoyed the same things he did, but in a purely consensual manner. My crimes were nothing compared to his, but I still wouldn't consider myself to be a good man.

Once I took over this place, I made a lot of changes. You couldn't walk inside unless you were twenty-one years of age. We had a strict security system that inhibited date-rape of any kind. If a woman said no, she said no. End of story.

Other than that, members were free to do whatever they wished.

What I loved most about Ruin was the freedom. I could be exactly who I was without shame. When I walked up to a woman and told her I wanted to spank her ass until it was red and irritated, she'd simply smile. When I'd tell her I wanted to suspend her from the ceiling, she'd extend her wrists and wait for the chains.

There was no judgment.

So this place was a safe haven for me.

A place where I felt most alive.

But having Rome in my life complicated things. I truly believed I could bring her here eventually. But now that she told me she loved me, said it with such conviction that I actually felt guilty for not saying it back, I wasn't sure how likely that was.

I had to choose.

Could I really keep running Ruin while I had this special kind of relationship with Rome? Shouldn't she know about it right now? Shouldn't she know where I went at night when she didn't sleep over? She trusted me, and now I felt dishonest for not telling her who I really was.

I had to tell her the truth or step away from Ruin.

And I knew I couldn't step away from Ruin. My soul was in this place. It'd been a part of my life forever.

So, that meant I had to tell Rome the truth.

I rested my fingertips against my lips as I considered it, unsure how I would even begin to explain my world to Rome — Vanilla. Would she judge me like everyone else? Or did she love me enough to keep an open mind? She allowed me to do some kinky stuff to her, so she definitely could expand her horizons.

I knew she trusted me, so hopefully, that trust was enough.

I was going to go through with it.

Come clean.

Fuck, I hoped it went well. Losing her wasn't an option. We'd made so much progress, and I didn't want to give it up. I wanted to move forward with her, have a life that we could both enjoy.

My office door burst open when Jackson walked inside. He may have knocked, but the music was so loud I couldn't hear it. The music from the club doubled in sound once the door was open. When he shut it behind him, it returned to a dull hum.

"Hey, I've got a new member in the hallway. Wants to join."

"We're at full capacity." Now that Rome had been chased from my thoughts, I focused all my attention on him.

"He's just one more. I really like the guy, and he's willing to pay double the membership fee."

"We're at full capacity," I repeated in a bored voice. Jackson and I had already had this discussion. If we let this business go to shit, we would lose members just as quickly as we received new ones.

"Come on, it's one more person." He rested his hands on my desk and leaned forward. "Is one person that big of a deal?"

"If we make an exception for him, we have to make an exception for other people."

"Oh, come on. The front door says we aren't accepting new members. The only reason why this guy asked is because I know him."

Jackson would pester me until he got his way, or he would just do it behind my back. I had bigger issues on my plate, and this didn't deserve more energy than necessary. "Fine. Send him in."

"Yes!" He fist-pumped the air and ran back to the door.

The second he was gone, I thought about Rome

again, unsure when I was going to confess my darkest secret to her. I wanted to sleep with her a few more times, just in case she walked away. But even if I did get in a few more rounds, I would never be satisfied—because I'd always want her.

"Here he is." Jackson walked back inside with his friend behind him. "This is Christopher. Christopher, this is my brother and co-owner of Ruin." He stepped aside so we could shake hands.

I stared into the face of a man I already knew—and had known for a while. He stared at me with the same threatened expression, cold and surprised. His arms remained by his sides as his expression darkened, turning into a look of dark rage.

Fuck.

I rose to my full height and tried to think of a quick explanation, a way to defuse the bloodlust on his face.

Christopher didn't say a word, looking at me like a bug stuck on the bottom of his shoe. He liked me, even respected me, but now that he knew I operated the most popular BDSM club in New York, he despised me. He could only assume that I was the biggest liar on the planet.

Jackson glanced back and forth between us. "Do you two know each other?"

Christopher stepped forward, his hands still by his

sides. He snorted through his nose then spit on my desk, covering the top of my laptop. His eyes never left my face. "No. Not anymore." He left my office and stormed out, leaving the door open as he walked away.

I dropped back into the chair and dragged my hands down my face, knowing the first thing he would do was return home and tell Rome everything. She would hear the terrible news from him, that I'd been lying to her this entire time.

I was in deep shit.

Jackson turned back to me once Christopher was gone. "What the hell was that about?"

I dropped my hands into my lap, feeling cold panic sweep over me. "That was Rome's brother."

"Seriously?" he asked, his jaw dropping.

I nodded.

"Oh, damn. He's nothing like her."

"No, he's not. And now he's going to let my skeletons out of the closet."

Jackson didn't show any sympathy. "Well, you've had six months to tell her the truth. It's not like you didn't have a chance."

I glared at him. "Thanks, Jackson. You're such a comfort…"

He shrugged in apology. "I want my brother back. And the sooner she leaves, the sooner you'll be back to normal. You don't know what I'm talking about, but very soon, you will."

It was hard for me to imagine being with another woman after Rome. She was the only woman I wanted to spank and fuck. She was the only woman I allowed to sleep in my bed. She was the only woman who ever met my mother. The future was dark and cold, and I loathed my next conversation with Rome.

If she even gave me a conversation.

11

CALLOWAY

I knew I was walking into a war zone when I went to her apartment. Christopher would probably punch me in the face, and I wouldn't block the hit because I deserved it. It would be easier to call, but that would also be pussy shit.

I wanted to talk face-to-face.

I knocked on the door and heard Christopher's voice from the living room. "Gee, I wonder who that could be?" He yanked the door open and stared me down with the same expression he wore at Ruin. If he'd had a gun, he probably would have shot me right then and there. "Come here to tell us some more lies? To make us believe you're something you're not." He pushed the door open until it banged against the wall. "Get your ass inside, and tell us all about it."

I hated being told what to do. It rubbed me the

wrong way and set my teeth on edge. My automatic response was to grab him by the neck and slam his head against the wall. But since that wouldn't help my chances with Rome, I kept my hands to myself.

I walked inside and saw her standing in the living room, her arms crossed over her chest. She wore an old t-shirt and sweatpants, her hair in a bun because she'd already been in bed when Christopher came home and told her the news.

The look she gave me was terrifying.

So much rage. So much hate.

All directed at me.

Christopher slammed the door once I was inside. "Tell her the truth, Calloway Owens...if that's even your real name. She needs to hear it from you." He raised a hand to my shoulder to shove me.

That was something I wouldn't allow. I grabbed his wrist before he could touch me, warning him with my gaze. "I get that you're upset. But don't fucking touch me." I pushed his hand back, forcing him to stagger slightly. I liked Christopher and didn't want to throw a punch, but if he pushed me, I would snap.

"Calloway." Rome's commanding voice came into my ear, making me forget about my standoff with Christopher. There was strength but also a noticeable hint of betrayal.

I turned my gaze on her, seeing the unrelenting fire in her eyes. Her eyes shifted back and forth as she looked into my gaze, searching for the truth without asking a single question. Her arms were still tightly crossed over her chest, her walls higher than they were when we first met. I actually felt a sense of fear jolt through me because the idea of losing her was oddly terrifying.

"I'm gonna give you the benefit of the doubt after everything we've been through." Even in sweats and a loose bun, she looked ready to attend the Oscars. Her natural confidence was her most beautiful feature. Despite what her brother had witnessed, she was still giving me a chance to tell my side of the story. It made me want her more. "Is everything Christopher told me true? Are you the owner of a BDSM club?" Her voice shook at the end, like the word BDSM was a curse.

I held her gaze and felt my heart sink into my stomach. Judging by the look on her face, once I gave my answer, she would be done with me. It was as clear as the sky on a cloudless day. "Christopher, can I speak to Rome alone?"

"Fuck no," he barked. "I have no idea who you are."

"Christopher, it's fine," Rome whispered. "Perhaps we should have this conversation in private."

Once Rome asked him to leave, Christopher didn't

object. He walked to the door. "I'm just a phone call away…" His footsteps sounded against the hardwood floor, and then the door clicked shut behind him.

My eyes never left her face. These past six months had been the best of my life. I wasn't ready to walk away.

"Calloway?" she pressed. "Answer my question."

I ran my hand across my hair and over the back of my neck, wanting to give the answer she wanted to hear —but that also wasn't a lie. "Yes." I lowered my hand and rested it by my side. "I've been running it for seven years now. It belonged to my father, and he handed it down to me."

She tightened her arms, taking a deep breath like the answer was painful to hear. "I can only assume you haven't told me this because you're involved with the lifestyle…" It wasn't truly a question because she obviously didn't want to hear the answer. "You knew I would disapprove."

"No."

When she turned her eyes back on me, there was a small gleam of hope.

"I was going to tell you. Actually, I was planning on talking to you this week. The timing of this nightmare was just poor."

"Why did you wait so long to tell me the truth?"

Here was the difficult part. I had no idea how she would react. "Because I want you to live in my world too. I knew you weren't ready for that over the past six months. I was waiting until I thought you would consider it."

"Consider what?" she asked.

I slid my hands into my pockets, knowing this was the moment of truth. "Being my sub."

Her face held the exact same expression, a cold exterior that couldn't be penetrated. She wasn't as angry as I expected her to be. To find out her boyfriend was sitting inside a sex club while she slept would piss off anyone.

I wasn't sure if she even knew what a sub was. "I'm a Dom, Rome. I've inherited this trait from my father, and I can't shake it. I know I'm never going to change. I was hoping we could have that kind of relationship. If you need more time, I understand. But I hope you don't reject the idea altogether."

Like she was talking to herself, she whispered under her breath. "Now it all makes sense…"

I still couldn't gauge her reaction. She didn't seem angry. But she didn't seem happy either.

She chuckled in a sarcastic way, even though there was nothing funny about this situation. "I knew you were too good to be true. An alarm kept going off in my head, saying there must be something wrong with you...and there is."

The insult stung me—right in the chest. Like everyone else, she thought I was a freak. I'd hoped she would keep an open mind, but it didn't seem like it would happen.

"I'm not even mad," she continued. "First Hank and now you..." She shook her head. "I have terrible taste in men. I officially give up. Being single with a bunch of cats doesn't sound half bad anymore."

"I don't know Hank, but I assure you, I'm nothing like him." My jaw clenched tightly at the comparison. I never wanted her to think about another guy when we were together. Hank was probably an asshole, but I genuinely cared about Rome.

"Actually, you're exactly alike," she whispered. "And I feel like an idiot for not noticing."

"I didn't mean—"

"I gave you my virginity." She laughed again, but tears formed in her eyes. "I told you I loved you. I accepted your job offer to be closer to you. I feel..." She closed her eyes for a moment before she reopened them. "I feel so stupid."

I felt like shit.

Worse than shit.

I hated myself.

No, I loathed myself.

"Rome, it wasn't like that. I care about you—a lot. The second I saw you in that bar, I knew I had to have you. For the past six months, I've been absolutely faithful to you. I haven't even looked at another woman. I've been in this relationship completely—heart, body, mind, and soul. I meant every word I said to you."

"I'm sorry, Calloway," she said in a resigned voice. "You had ulterior motives throughout this entire relationship. I don't exactly trust anything you say right now."

Fuck, that hurt.

It hurt more because I deserved it.

"I've never lied to you. I just didn't tell you this one aspect of my life. I wanted to wait until I thought you were ready to hear it."

"No, you purposely kept me in the dark for six months. You misled me about the man you really are. You didn't tell me about your sexual preferences, calling me Vanilla like it was cute. Maybe you never directly lied because I never questioned you about it, but this is worse. I don't know what's real and what's not real."

This was going much worse than I'd ever imagined. I thought she wouldn't agree to be my sub, but I didn't think she would write off our entire relationship as meaningless. That wasn't how I felt at all. "Sweetheart, it's not like that… I've loved every moment with you. I don't want to be with anyone else."

"Even if that's true, it doesn't change the fact that you hurt me—so much." She stepped back, putting more space between us. "Because I was invested in this relationship and hoping it would last forever. But you already knew the end before the beginning."

"In my defense, I told you I wasn't looking for marriage and a happily ever after." Maybe she didn't believe me at the time, but I meant it. "I said that right in the beginning so you wouldn't get your hopes up."

She held my gaze, the memory on the surface of her eyes. "Christopher told me to ignore it…"

"Why would he say such a thing?"

"Because he said every guy says that exact same thing…until they find the woman they can't live without."

A pain thudded in my chest, hot and cold at the same time. I didn't understand the sensation or what it meant. All I knew was I felt it.

"Obviously, he was wrong… I was wrong."

"Rome, you're looking at this the wrong way. I do want this to last forever. I just want our relationship to be a little different. That's all."

"You mean, you want to hurt me." She broke eye contact because she couldn't look at me anymore. "You want to tie me up and knock me around. Yeah, that sounds like a blast... I'll pass."

"It's not like that." Not even close. "All the things we've already done are precursors to that. You would enjoy it. You would enjoy me. I promise you."

"No, I don't enjoy being bossed around. Come on, Calloway." She turned back to me, a sneer on her face. "Do you even know me?"

The insult burned through my skin. "Yes, I do know you. I know how much it turned you on when you slapped me—both times. I know how much you liked my cock in your ass. I know how much you like it when I give commands when we're in the bedroom. Stop looking at this in black and white. Give it a chance, Rome."

"No." She shook her head, resistance in her eyes. "I've already been down this road before. I'm not going there again. You would have saved me a lot of time and heartbreak if you'd just had the balls to be honest with me."

I only focused on the first thing she said. "You've been down this road before?" How could she have been part of the lifestyle if she was a virgin? "What does that mean, Rome?"

She sighed as if she wasn't sure she wanted to explain the story.

"Tell me." I kept my tone polite so I wouldn't push her further away. I would always be authoritative, but fortunately, I was able to control it around her—for the most part.

"When I first graduated college, I moved to New York for work. I had mounds of student loans to pay without any way of paying them. I lived in a studio apartment with three other girls for a while. I couldn't find a job that paid enough, and eventually, I wound up living on the street. Christopher was in the same position I was for a while because he didn't have a dollar to his name while he was doing an internship."

Now I wished I'd never asked. Imagining her in a sleeping bag on the sidewalk made me hate myself for living in my mansion. I wanted to take care of her. I wished I could go back in time and take her home, lavishing her in warm clothes, food, and anything else she wanted.

"One day, this nice man walked up to me and gave me a hundred bucks. I was so grateful I cried. He set me up in one of the apartment complexes he owned so I would have a place to stay with Christopher. Once things were settled, he asked me out. I thought he was cute and compassionate, so of course, I said yes. But then he asked me to do things I wasn't ready for. I said no, and he accepted that—for a while. But then he became angry when he didn't get his way, threatening to take away everything he'd given me. When I refused to sleep with him, he broke my arm and beat me senseless..."

Tears sprang to my eyes, burning them because my ducts hadn't produced liquid in so long. The idea of Rome suffering made me break inside. The fact that a man took advantage of her when she had nothing left in the world just sickened me.

"He wanted me to submit to him. He wanted to control me. He enjoyed hurting me. The gleam in his eyes when he heard my bone crack in two...is something I'll never forget." She stared at the ground as she finished her story. "So, I'll never be your sub, Calloway. I've been used and abused once before, and I won't tolerate it ever again."

I had to walk away because the pain was too much. I couldn't face her any longer, not when I felt my body slowly begin to crack. I turned away and approached the window in the living room, overlooking the traffic down below. My face was hidden, and my breathing was under control. But my momentary privacy allowed a tear to escape from the corner of my right eye, drip down my cheek, and fall to the floor.

I took a moment to center myself, not giving in to the overwhelming grief flooding through my body. I hadn't felt this way since I first admitted my mother to the nursing home. The idea of Rome being treated that way disgusted me—killed me.

I wasn't sure how long I stood there, but it seemed to be an eternity. I concentrated on breathing in and out, dispelling the agony and the rage within me. I needed to remain calm because going on a rampage wouldn't fix my current situation. What happened to Rome was in the past, and no matter how powerful I was, I couldn't change the past.

I could only change the future.

Once I put myself together enough to face her, I turned back around and walked to where she stood on the opposite side of the living room. She was exactly where I left her, her arms still crossed over her chest. Now she wore a defeated look, appearing hollow.

"There are a few things I'd like to say," I whispered. "I hope you'll hear me out."

The only response I got was eye contact.

"What he did to you…" I couldn't finish the sentence because the rage started back up again. "Is completely different from the kind of relationship I want. I would never hurt you, Rome. I would never do anything that you didn't explicitly want me to do. Our relationship would be about trust. I would give the commands, but you would have all the control. With just a single word, you can make me stop instantly. There would only be pleasure—I promise you."

She shook her head, the response I didn't want to see. "Christopher told me about the stuff he saw inside Ruin. Women with chains around their necks while men held on to them like dogs on a leash. The way the men won't even allow their women to speak in front of other men. The way they whip them in playrooms until their skin is bruised. As a feminist, I'm appalled that women participate in this world at all. I'm not ashamed to say I want true love. I want a man to love me with all his heart, to be gentle with me, to be satisfied when he makes love to me. I want a man who doesn't get off on hurting his woman." Her eyes burned as she looked at me. "Maybe you're into that, but I'm certainly not."

She didn't understand, and now I feared she never would. "You're looking at it from an outside point of view. That's not what it's really like."

"So you're saying the stuff Christopher told me is untrue?"

"Not at all." It was definitely true. I'd had a chain around Isabella's neck several times. "Yes, it happens every single day. But we don't have to do anything you don't want to do, Rome. You aren't listening to me."

"No," she scoffed. "You aren't listening to me. I

want nothing to do with your underworld, and I'm not going to change my mind."

I was losing her. "I may have the control, but you have all the power, sweetheart. I would never do anything that you didn't want me to do. Do you understand that? I would never put a chain around your neck unless you asked me to. I would never tell you to be silent in front of other Doms if you had something to say. You're missing the fact that this is all consensual. As in, both parties want it. You and I can have any kind of relationship you want. We already do stuff that I enjoy. I loved tying you up to my headboard, and I know you loved it too. So don't completely write this off because you don't understand it."

She only shook her head.

"Rome, please, just consider it."

"No," she said coldly. "You and I want different things. I'm never going to be your sub, Calloway. Accept it, and move on."

I bowed my head in disappointment, struggling to accept the truth. I wasn't getting my way with the one woman I truly wanted. "What if we took baby steps? What if we tried—"

"No." She turned her head away, no longer looking at me.

Our relationship had already progressed beyond

general lovemaking. I took her roughly in many ways. I asked her to do things for me, and she didn't even realize it. Her prejudice against this world was unfair. What Hank did to her was just physical assault—a crime. But it didn't seem like I could argue my point any further.

"I'll submit my resignation tomorrow morning."

I hadn't even considered our work relationship. "Please don't do that."

"I can't work with you every day, Calloway. No matter how much I may love my job."

I'd go crazy if I didn't have some kind of connection with her. If I never saw her again, I would lose my mind. "Rome, you're perfect for the position. Think of all the things you've done in the past month. The people of New York City need you. Please don't walk away because of me. It wouldn't be fair to everyone else."

"But I can't—"

"I can be professional, Rome. You and I are both mature adults who can handle this. Whether we're together or apart, we really do make a great team. Let's not ruin that."

She shut her mouth, having nothing to say in response. She loved her job. It was obvious every time I saw her in her office, every time she talked about a new project she was working on. She had the kind of compassion that was a necessity for Humanitarians United. Frankly, she was the most qualified person in the building.

At least I would get to see her every day—even if I didn't see her every night.

When she said nothing else, I assumed that meant she would stay on board. "I don't understand you, Calloway. I thought I did, but I really don't. How can you run a place like Ruin, and then go to work every day at a place like Humanitarians United? It's like you're two different people."

"Because I am two different people. I started Humanitarians United to balance out the terrible things my father did to innocent people who didn't have any way to fight him. I run it every day to offset the dark things I'm into... To make up for them."

She watched my expression, her thoughts a mystery.

Now there was nothing else for me to do besides walk away...but that seemed impossible. "I don't want this to end..."

"It has to. You and I want different things and neither one of us will change our minds."

No, I could never abandon who I really was. I could only fight it for short periods of time. And after Rome explained what had happened to her, I couldn't blame her for being afraid. I'd lied to her for the past six months. It didn't surprise me that her guard was up again.

"I just wish you had told me the truth, Calloway. Finding out from Christopher..." She didn't finish the sentence.

Earlier that evening, I'd decided to sit down and talk to her about everything. But to say that now would just be empty words. Now I had to walk out of this apartment and not look back. I'd have to look at her at work every day and know she was no longer mine. I'd have to sleep in my large bed alone, wishing she were beside me. I'd have to find a sub that could please me, but the idea of any woman but Rome nearly repulsed me. "I know."

12

CALLOWAY

The finality of the breakup didn't hit me until I got home.

Once I was inside my house and accepted that she wouldn't be joining me, I realized I was truly alone. My enormous bed upstairs would feel twice as big without a person to share it with. I would only cook dinner for one each night. When I sat on the couch and watched TV, she wouldn't lie on my chest, her hair brushing against my neck.

Rome was really gone.

My first instinct was to head to the liquor cabinet.

And drink away my sorrow.

I sat at the kitchen table and faced my backyard, placing the bottle of scotch and the glass on the table. I stared at the label before I poured myself a drink and swirled the ice cubes. Then I downed it in a single gulp, feeling the fire move down my throat all the way into my stomach.

"Fuck." I leaned over the table and rubbed my temple, realizing I hadn't hit a low point like this for six months. One of the first times she slept over, I had a nightmare and tried to drink myself into a stupor. But that woman told me to shove my drinks up my ass and get over it.

I already missed her.

I thought about the course of our relationship and wondered what I could have done to save it. If I'd told her the truth sooner, would she still be in my life? If I had walked away from Ruin before Christopher appeared, could I have given her the life she wanted? So many different possibilities, but all of them led to the same destination.

Losing her.

I had been happy with Isabella until I spotted Rome in that bar. Once I broke it off with Isabella, I didn't feel anything for her. There was no pain, no regret. Like it had never happened, it was hardly a memory.

But with Rome, I felt like I'd died a million deaths.

It was pure agony.

I'd never felt this terrible — not once.

I pulled out my phone, and without really thinking, I called Jackson.

"So, what happened?" he barked the second he took the call. "Did Christopher rat you out?"

"Of course he did." I poured another glass, spilling drops of scotch onto the table. "Told Rome everything."

"And?"

"She left me." The words hurt to say out loud. It was far worse than saying it in my head. I closed my eyes and felt my temple thud with a migraine.

Jackson picked up on my resigned tone. He didn't gloat or even seem happy. It was one of the rare times he actually showed compassion. "Sorry, man..."

I didn't have any friends because I preferred solitude. Acquaintances were easier, much simpler. Friendships required expectations, and expectations always led to disappointments. And disappointments led to reevaluation of said friendships. So, Jackson was all I had. "She doesn't want anything to do with our lifestyle. I have no choice but to accept it."

"It sucks right now, but you'll get through it, Cal."

Would I? This feeling in my stomach was new. I felt sick.

"Are you drinking?"

"What else would I be doing?" I downed the shot and slammed the glass onto the surface of the wood.

"Want me to come by?"

"No." I sat in the darkness and looked out the window, listening to the memory of Rome's laugh in my ears.

"You know...if this woman is different, maybe you should try the vanilla route. You wouldn't be the first." Jackson spent so much time giving me shit for turning my back on Ruin, and now he was encouraging me to do it.

"We both know I couldn't do it—at least not forever." Something would give eventually. I would have to break it off and hurt her because she refused to allow me to tie her up. I'd have to find someone who would allow me to do it instead.

"I'm sorry," he said for the third time. "Is there anything I can do?"

I eyed the scotch, seeing that it was half empty. "No. There's nothing anyone can do for me."

I didn't sleep that night.

I stayed at the dining table, drunk out of my mind. When the sun rose the next morning and peeked through my blinds, I wasn't entirely sober. But I wasn't wasted either. I had a hot shower then threw on the first suit I could find.

I looked forward to seeing Rome at the office. A stupid part of me hoped she would have reconsidered overnight and had decided to give us another chance. But the pragmatic man inside me knew there was no possibility of that ever happening.

So now I dreaded it.

I wouldn't have to interact with her often, but there was always a possibility I would see her on a regular basis. Maybe we would pass each other in the hallway on the way to lunch. Maybe she would be in the conference room with her team as I walked by. There were endless scenarios in which my eyes could fall on her.

I arrived at the office later than usual and grabbed my messages from my secretary. I didn't spot Rome in the hallway, and I purposely didn't walk past her office. Once I was behind my black doors and had plenty of privacy, I pinched the bridge of my nose between my fingers, releasing a sigh that carried my pain.

I needed to snap out of this.

Rome was just a woman.

They came and went.

I shook it off and got to work, but my focus only

lasted an hour at the most. My thoughts drifted back to that busty brunette with those long legs running through my mind. I didn't just miss having her in my bed because the sex was great. I missed holding her, brushing my lips against her soft hair. I missed telling her about my day, telling her things I never told anyone else.

It felt like I'd lost a friend.

The end of the day couldn't come soon enough. I was eager to leave the office space I shared with her. Pretending everything was fine to everyone I talked to was much more difficult than I thought it was going to be.

When I finally left for the day, I felt some of the stress leave my shoulders. I walked to the elevators and happened to catch one right when the doors opened. I stepped inside and hit the lobby button.

Because I was the unluckiest man in the world, Rome rounded the corner, obviously leaving for the day too. She stopped when she saw me, her eyes immediately glued to mine. It didn't seem like she was going to take the elevator, but it would be stupid for her not to. She could easily have to wait ten minutes for the next one.

I held the door open and nodded for her to come inside.

She tightened her purse over her shoulder like I might snatch it and walked inside.

I released the door and returned to my side of the elevator, my hands resting in my pockets.

The elevator began to move, and it was the tensest two minutes of my life.

Rome looked at anything but me, keeping her eyes trained on the metal door in front of her. She pulled her hair over one shoulder, trying to block her face from my view. Her perfume filled the small space, hinting of flowers in summer.

I missed her even more now.

I wanted to say something, but I wasn't sure if it was too soon. Was it better just to stay quiet? Should I say hello? Was it more or less awkward to say something? "I got your budget reports. I approved everything you asked for." It wouldn't be smart to talk about our relationship, not when we'd just broken up twenty-four hours ago. But talking about work was safe. It was better than not saying anything at all.

"That's great." Her beautiful voice came out quiet. "Thank you."

"I have a few potential donors on my line. If we snag them, we can do more this year. We'll see."

She nodded but didn't say anything.

Once the elevator came to a stop and the doors

opened, she walked out first. "I'll see you tomorrow, Mr. Owens."

Mr. Owens.

I fucking hated it when she called me that. So impersonal. So meaningless. I was so much more to her than Mr. Fucking Owens. "Have a good night, Rome." I wasn't embarrassed to admit I stared at her ass as she walked away, watching it shift from side to side in her tight dress.

I'd probably beat off to the image tonight.

The second I got home, I hit the bottle again.

It's not like I had anything else to do.

My liquor cabinet was impressive because I collected fine wines and aged scotch. Sometimes bourbon and whiskey were in the mix. Ironically, I didn't care for beer. Far too weak for what I was used to.

A knock sounded on my front door, my hopes immediately jumping to finding one person standing there.

Rome.

Only she and Jackson knew where I lived. And it

was unlikely that Jackson had decided to show up at my door.

I opened the front door without even bothering to check who was on the other side. I wanted to come face-to-face with the beautiful woman who was constantly on my mind. I wanted to hear her say she would accept me for who I was and that we would work it out somehow.

But it was Christopher.

Looking just as pissed as before.

And Rome wasn't with him.

"I'm not gonna punch you in the face." He crossed his arms over his chest. "But if you say something, I might change my mind."

My disappointment swelled into my lungs and spread into my stomach. He was the last person I cared to see. "What do you want, Christopher?"

"What are you going to do about the apartment? I can get out within a month, but Rome is gonna have to go somewhere else. There won't be room for her."

"You guys are staying put." Even if she wasn't mine to take care of, I liked knowing she was safe. "I don't want the apartment. Keep it."

His anger never faded. "Is that supposed to make me like you?"

"No. I can tell your hatred is here to stay."

"Damn right it is." He dropped his arms to his sides then cracked his knuckles. "You're such a fucking asshole. You've got a lot of nerve."

"You're one to talk," I snapped. "You're the one who wanted to join Ruin." If he was gonna judge me, then his record better be squeaky clean.

He held up his finger like he was making a point. "I'm a single guy who can do whatever he wants. I've always been up front about my true colors with women. If you're into that kinky shit, I don't give a damn. But you swept Rome off her feet by pretending to be this compassionate humanitarian, and it was just a bunch of bullshit. That's unforgivable, Cal. And we both know it."

"I am a compassionate humanitarian. But I'm also into Ruin."

"I can only imagine the shit you did behind Rome's back every night she was sleeping down the hall from my bedroom. You're a piece of shit. I would kill you if I could get away with it."

I knew he meant it. "Christopher, I ran the business, but I never betrayed Rome. My hands were kept to myself. I never even looked at another woman."

He stared me down, his expression cold.

"I know you believe me." It was a gut instinct, a sense I could feel. "I was happy with Rome and never needed anyone else. My brother Jackson is too stupid to be in charge, so I need to do it. Yes, I'm a Dom and I usually have a sub, but I haven't participated in that lifestyle since the day I met your sister."

When Christopher was quiet, I knew he'd heard the sincerity in my voice.

"I miss her." I normally wouldn't say that to another guy, but I was at my lowest point. "I miss her like crazy, and I wish we could work this out. But she wants nothing to do with me — and I respect that."

"Why didn't you just tell her?"

"I was going to. I was just waiting for the right time."

"And there was no other opportunity in the past six months?" he asked incredulously.

"I just didn't think she was ready." I wouldn't go into details about my relationship with Rome. She wasn't really his sister, but it was still awkward to talk about. "She told me about Hank, and frankly, I can't blame her for feeling this way."

His eyebrow rose. "She told you about Hank?"

I nodded, feeling my blood boil when I remembered her story. "That he broke her arm in two different places because she wouldn't sleep with him."

He kept staring at me like I might say something else. "Did she talk about anything else?"

"No." Was there more?

Christopher ran his hands through his dark hair, his eyes cryptic. "If you're cool with it, then we're gonna stay put. We just moved in, and it would be a bitch to pack everything up again."

"Keep it." I just wished I could give the place to Rome instead. I wished I could make up a fake lottery and give her more money than she knew what to do with. She was already a powerful woman, but I wanted to give her more power. I wanted her to be above everyone else, where no one would even consider laying a hand on her. If I could give her a crown, I would.

"Thanks..." He placed his hands in his pockets and stepped back slightly. "So...I guess this is it."

My misery derived from losing Rome, but I felt an ache from losing Christopher too. I considered him to be a friend, not just her brother. "Yeah...I guess so."

He extended his hand to shake mine.

I eyed it, touched by the gesture. Despite how angry he was with me, he still had some affection for me. I shook his hand.

"I don't really understand what happened with Rome, but I can tell you really care about her."

"More than you know." I lowered my hand and cleared my throat.

"Good luck." He gave me a curt nod before he

walked off my porch and headed to the sidewalk. He didn't turn back as he walked away, his hands stuffed into his pockets to hide away from the cold.

I watched him go, feeling Rome walk out of my life all over again.

When his shadow was gone, I walked back inside and headed straight for the liquor.

13

ROME

Christopher watched me like a hawk every single day. He didn't go on dates or hang out with his work buddies. He didn't play video games either, choosing to watch whatever I was watching on TV. He didn't ask me a lot of questions, but he stuck to my side like I might crumble.

Yes, losing Calloway was hard.

Knowing he'd lied to me was harder.

Seeing him every day at work was heartbreaking.

But I wasn't going to shed a tear. I wasn't going to give in to the pain. I wasn't going to let my life slip away. Calloway hurt me in so many ways, I didn't know where to begin. He was purposely deceitful, and I felt stupid for trusting that man. So, if I let him tear me down the way Hank did, I would let Calloway win.

I couldn't let him win.

I made a sandwich then sat on the other couch, ignoring Christopher's peering gaze. I wasn't sure if he was trying to be discreet or not, but his constant worry was as obvious as the sun.

He finally snapped and turned off the TV. "Look, we need to talk."

"About?" I popped a chip into my mouth and ate it slowly.

"I know what you're doing, and it's not gonna work."

"I'm just eating a sandwich. What do you think I'm doing?"

"Don't be a smartass right now." He leaned forward, resting his forearms on his knees. "Ever since you guys broke up, you've acted like everything is fine, like nothing has changed. But everything has changed, Rome. You can't just ignore the pain and forget the relationship ever happened."

"I appreciate your concern." I kept my voice calm, trying to make him relax. "But really, I'm fine. Calloway lied to me and hurt me… I'm not gonna say he didn't. But I'm also not gonna sit around and cry all day. That's not me, and we both know it."

"I think ignoring it altogether isn't good either."

"I'm fine." I knew I was lying to myself, but if I lied enough times, maybe it would become true.

He sighed then leaned back into the couch. "He's a complete mess."

I was about to take a bite of my sandwich when I changed my mind. "You've seen him?"

He nodded. "A few nights ago."

"Why? Where?"

"I went to his place and gave him a piece of my mind."

Oh, great. "Christopher…he's not worth it."

"Too late. I already told him off."

"How did you even know where he lived?"

"Because I'm not an idiot and can figure shit out." He crossed his arms, his eyebrows furrowed and tense. "And after I finished giving him hell, I actually felt bad for him."

"Don't." Calloway didn't deserve any sympathy.

"I know my opinion doesn't matter, but despite what he did, I think he really cares about you."

I didn't care how Calloway felt. He didn't prove it to me when he lied for so long—and about something so big. He liked chains and whips and for women to submit like slaves. I couldn't be more different, with a back so strong and rigid it would never bend—not even for him. "He had an odd way of showing it."

Christopher gave me a sad look, falling silent.

I felt stupid for giving Calloway so much of myself.

Not just my virginity, but my heart. I told him I loved him, and up until last week, I thought he felt the same way—even if he wouldn't say it. I felt a special connection with him, a partnership that could last a lifetime. He was my best friend, and I felt like I'd lost more than just a boyfriend.

If I thought about it too long, the depression would start to grow and pull me under. So, I concentrated on my sandwich and changed the subject. "Are you going to keep going to Ruin?"

He shook his head. "Major conflict of interest."

"I don't care if you do, Christopher."

"I know. But I'm still not interested. There're lots of other kink clubs in the city. If I get bored, I can explore one of those." He finally pulled his gaze away from my face, not staring at me so intently. "So…are you going to keep working with him?"

I told myself I could do it, that I could see him every day and still hold my head high, but when I spotted him in the hallway or the elevator, my heart fell into my stomach. "I really love my job, and I'm never going to find anything else like it."

"I guess that's a yes, then."

"He asked me to stay because he thinks I'm the best person for the job. He hasn't mentioned our relationship once while we've been at work. It seems to be working well enough. I guess I thought he might try to chase me...but he hasn't."

Christopher turned his gaze back to my face. "You sound disappointed."

"I'm not."

He gave me that knowing look, like he could see something written on my face. "Can you really not be with him? Or are you just mad at him?"

"What are you asking?" I didn't have a clue what kind of point he was trying to make.

"I'm asking exactly what I asked. Do you really not want to be with Calloway, or do you just need a break? Two completely different things."

"No. I can't be with him." It was as simple as that.

"Even though you love him?"

"He doesn't love me, remember?"

"Maybe he doesn't. But maybe he does."

I eyed him suspiciously. "What are you saying, Christopher?"

"I don't know... I know what he did was bad, but I still like him, you know? There's something about him, something so endearing."

Obviously. Why else would I have fallen in love with him so quickly? "Yes, he's very charismatic."

"I guess I sympathize with the guy because we really aren't that different."

"Yes, you are." Night and day.

"Look, I'm a pig just like him. I like kinky shit and loose chicks. But I know if the right woman came along, I'd cut out all the bullshit and be the man she deserved. Maybe he was part of that lifestyle. That doesn't make him a bad guy."

Christopher didn't know the whole story. "It's more complicated than that."

"How?"

"Look, you don't want to know this stuff, Christopher. I appreciate your concern, but it's misplaced."

"Why would I ask if I didn't want to know?" he asked.

"Because it's personal stuff. I don't want to know about your lady friends."

"Yeah, because that's all sex. What you had with Calloway was different. So, talk to me." He snapped his fingers. "I'm all ears, no judgments. I'm not gonna throw up or tease you about anything."

I knew he meant well, so I went for it. "Not only is it a problem that Calloway lied to me. But he doesn't want to give up what he does."

His eyebrows furrowed, unsure what I meant. "Which is?"

"He wants to be my Dom. That's what he's wanted

from the beginning. He said he wanted to break me in before he pushed me that far. That's why he didn't tell me the truth for so long—afraid of scaring me off."

"Oh…" Christopher nodded in understanding.

"And I want nothing to do with that lifestyle. It's not who I am or what I stand for. I don't want a man who needs to smack me around to get off."

He nodded again. "And he's unwilling to walk away?"

"He says it's who he is—and he's not gonna change."

Christopher's eyes moved to the floor, his melancholy increasing. "I would believe that, but some parts aren't adding up… Why would he be with you for six months, giving up that lifestyle, if he couldn't give it up forever?"

The idea had been sitting in the back of my mind for a long time. I didn't want to think about it because it hurt too much. The truth was enough to finally break me down, to make me convulse with agony. "Because he never gave it up. All those nights when he was there and I was here… Who knows what he was really doing."

"I asked him about that. He said he was always faithful to you."

"But how can we really believe him?" I whispered. "I don't think we can."

Christopher fell silent, caressing his knuckles. "You knew him better than I did, but he seems like a pretty loyal man."

"No, I didn't know him better than you did." I didn't know him at all.

———

As the week passed, working with him every day got easier. I really didn't see him that often. There were days when I didn't even hear his name. I stayed inside my office and took care of my work, and a lot of the time, I was out in the city doing research. I was surveying different communities of the homeless, determining which group needed what kind of care. Those afternoons when I was outside were the best.

It was the only time I didn't think about him.

Calloway had already approved my budget for the next six months, but I had to decide how it would be allocated. As time passed, different needs arose. I couldn't predict everything so far in advance. Unfortunately, a terrible flu had swept through, and a lot of homeless people died because they weren't given the care they needed.

Therefore, funds needed to be moved to vaccinations.

It wasn't built into my budget report. So I needed to ask for an approval of a higher budget, or I'd have to take away different expenses, which I wanted to avoid. It wasn't easy to take away food and warm clothing when those things were just as essential as medicine.

Instead of talking to him face-to-face, I emailed Calloway. Just seeing his name in the address field sent my heart into my stomach. I was so disappointed in him for how much he'd hurt me and because he wasn't willing to fight to get me back. Perhaps if he gave up Ruin and the dirty shit he was into, we could work it out. But he'd made it clear he wouldn't change his mind. Good sex took precedence over sensual lovemaking.

That probably hurt most of all.

His assistant called my office phone. "Mr. Owens would like to see you in his office."

My blood ran cold. I knew it was about the email I'd just sent out. It wasn't thorough enough, and he wanted to question me. So far, he hadn't mentioned our relationship while we were at work together, so I assumed I was probably safe. But being alone in his office would still be tense. "I'll be right there."

I walked down the hallway and past his assistant's desk as I headed to the enormous black doors. When I touched the knob, the metal felt ice-cold, just like his crystal blue eyes. I took a deep breath before I walked inside, finding him sitting behind his desk with his eyes on his screen. Normally, he was at the front of the room, close enough to touch me.

I walked inside and took a seat in one of the armchairs, trying to forget the way he'd held me in here just a few weeks earlier. He'd asked me to join him on a Saturday afternoon for a surprise, to meet his mother in an assisted-living facility. Our relationship seemed so tender, built on trust and so much more. And now we were strangers. "Did you want to talk about my request?"

"Yes." He closed out of whatever window he was looking at on his computer screen. He finally looked at me, showing no emotion other than indifference. He hadn't shaved in days, and his stubble had grown into a short beard. His blue eyes didn't seem as bright, like a cloud obscured their natural brilliance. When he looked at me, there was nothing there—just painful acceptance. "I've done some digging, and I haven't found any reports about the epidemic you're referring to."

"The news stations aren't reporting it. It's not something the general public cares about." Homeless people were at the bottom of the barrel, even if a lot of them were war veterans.

"Then how did you come across it?" He tilted his

head slightly, one hand resting on the desk. His knuckles were chiseled, and his veins were corded. He had the most masculine hands I'd ever seen. I missed the way they used to touch me.

"I know my city, Mr. Owens. I know my people."

He sighed in frustration, like I'd said something that upset him. "Don't call me that unless we're in public."

I didn't understand why his name was so offensive, but I didn't ask.

"If your information is true, then this is our priority. But I'm going to need to see some evidence."

"How?"

"Show me."

He wanted me to take him to the different gatherings of the homeless, the ones under the bridges, the ones at the east side of the park, and all the smaller communities scattered across the city. Just him and me. "Sure. Let me know when you're ready."

"I'm ready now." He rose from his chair, coming to his full height. With an expensive watch on his wrist and the black ring on his right hand, he looked like my deepest fantasy. With long legs and powerful arms, he was scorching in his suit. He always made me feel safe even when I didn't need protection.

I got lost in my thoughts and quickly shook it off, not wanting to make it obvious I was remembering all the nights we'd gotten naked together in his bed. I could feel the way his teeth nicked against my neck when he kissed me, if I closed my eyes and pictured it hard enough. "Do you want me to bring along anyone else?" So we won't be alone together?

"Your call." He straightened his suit and headed for the door, staying at least five feet away from me. "But make it quick. I have a lot of work to do."

I hadn't spent this much time with Calloway since we went our separate ways. We took cabs to different parts of the city, and once we approached the homeless communities, Calloway knew my information was accurate.

Without taking swabs or running labs, it was obvious the flu had spread to nearly everyone. They were already outside in the cold all day long, so their chances of fighting off the illness were minimal.

When we approached a group, Calloway took the lead and spoke to the men and women as equals, looking them in the eye and even shaking their hands. He pulled out all the cash he had and handed it off to a war veteran who had lost his leg. Like possessions meant nothing to him, he gave everything away.

That was the man I'd fallen in love with.

He kept one eye on me the entire time, coming back to my side when the men stared at me a moment longer than they should. I wasn't afraid in the least, but Calloway's protectiveness would never die.

"I think we're done here." Calloway came to my side, and his arm immediately wrapped around my waist.

I stilled at the touch.

"Let's get a cab," he said into my ear. "Come on."

I moved with him but still felt uneasy with his hand on me. It was warm and soothing, carrying memories of beautiful nights. But it was also painful, full of affection that I could never receive freely.

He waved down a cab and got me inside before he scooted into the seat beside me. He gave the address to the office, and the cab drove off. The sun had nearly set, and night descended on New York City. Calloway stared out the window the entire drive back, not explaining our sudden departure.

"What's wrong?"

"One of the men wouldn't stop looking at you. Made me uncomfortable."

"They wouldn't hurt me."

He turned his gaze on me, his look cold and unforgiving. "You don't know that, Rome. Never make that assumption. Just because they're poor and hungry doesn't mean they're saints. Don't make that mistake again." He looked out the window, dismissing the conversation.

"I can take care of myself, Calloway." I'd been doing it for a long time before he came along. I would do just fine without him. I'd lived on the streets, begged for food, and had a life just as hard as his. I saw the good in people because I knew it was there—along with all the bad.

He didn't look at me again. "I never said you couldn't."

"You implied it."

"I'm just giving you a lesson." He finally turned back to me, his jaw clenched. "By now, I would assume you've figured out that not all men are as they appear." His meaning was just as clear as crystal.

"I guess I'm a slow learner."

When we returned to the office, everyone had already left for the day. The lights were off, and the monitors were black. I went to my office and grabbed my things, pissed that Calloway had the nerve to say that to me— like he was the one who'd been wronged.

I hated him.

But I still loved him.

And that made me hate him more.

I darted to the elevator as quickly as I could, determined to get out of there so I wouldn't have to see his obnoxiously handsome face.

But he was already there—waiting for me. He hit the button, and the doors opened.

I hoped this wouldn't become a habit.

We got inside, and the elevator began its descent all the way down to the bottom floor.

I gripped the strap of my purse so tightly the skin of my palm turned red. I pretended this breakup didn't wound me as much as it did, but my anger just proved how devastated I was inside. I wanted more than an apology from him. I wanted more than he could possibly give.

"I'm sorry I let my anger get to me back there." His words broke the tension, slicing through it like a knife. "I haven't been myself lately. I haven't slept since…you left me."

His apology just made me angrier. "Poor thing, I made you lose sleep? It's not like I lost anything…" Bitterness escaped in my voice, thinking about all the things he took from me. Not only my virginity, but he made me believe in love and trust. Then he shattered them like some cruel joke.

He turned his head my way, the elevator still descending. "Everything I felt for you was real. It still is, Rome. You have no idea how much I miss you. You have no idea how much I hate that bed now that you aren't in it. Before you, I couldn't stand the thought of sleeping with anyone, and now, I can't sleep without you."

His confession tugged at my heartstrings, but I still didn't cave. "I'm sure you slept with all those subs at Ruin just fine…"

He slammed the STOP button with his face, bringing the elevator to an immediate halt.

"What the hell are you—"

He cornered me against the back wall, his arms pressed against the metal on either side of me so I couldn't hit the elevator buttons. "You are the only woman in my life, Rome. When I was at Ruin, I was in the office doing payroll, inventory, schedules, and other shit just as boring. Not once did I lay a hand on anyone else. I can accept you walking away, but I can't accept you believing that bullshit. Do you understand me?"

I kept my hands to my sides, seeing those smooth lips that I used to kiss over and over.

"Vanilla, do you understand me?" His hand moved

around my neck, and he squeezed me gently, his fingertips pulsing against my skin.

"Don't call me that."

"I'll call you whatever the hell I want. Now, answer me."

"I don't know what to think, Calloway."

He pressed his face closer to mine. "If I'd fucked someone else, I would tell you. I have nothing to hide. You know I own Ruin, and I feel no shame in that partnership. You were my whole world when we were together. Why would I look at the moon, when I have all the fucking stars right in front of me?" He finally released my neck but didn't step back. He kept me boxed in, away from the elevator buttons.

I believed him. He gave me no evidence of his claims, but I didn't need any more convincing. When he was this passionate, this angry, I knew he was being honest. "Okay."

"Okay, what?" he snarled.

"I believe you."

He finally stepped back, but he looked just as angry as when the conversation started. He slammed his hand onto the green button so the elevator would start back up. He leaned against the wall, not looking at me. He crossed his powerful arms over his chest as the hum of the elevator came back to life.

I remained in my spot, hardly breathing because so much electricity ran through my veins. The chemistry was exactly the same, unbelievably scorching. I felt my fingertips and toes burn from the heat.

He sighed then looked up at the fluorescent lights on the ceiling. "Sweetheart, it would be different with me... I would never hurt you."

I didn't expect him to fight for me. It was the first time he'd mentioned anything since we went our separate ways. A part of me was glad to see his unkempt beard and the exhaustion in his eyes. It made me feel important, that our relationship really did mean something to him. I could have sworn he loved me, with all those kisses and heated looks, but then I found out the terrible truth. I feared I didn't matter to him, that while I was madly in love with him, I was just some woman he would forget about. "You know I can't do it, Calloway."

"You trust me."

"I did trust you. Not anymore."

He kept his eyes on me. "I'm the same man you fell for. Nothing has changed. Just give me a chance."

"I don't want to be your sub, Calloway. I want to be your girlfriend—nothing else."

His eyes darkened, his thoughts unreadable.

"That's nonnegotiable."

"Are you saying you would take me back on those terms?"

I avoided his gaze, surprised by the question. "I don't know..."

"Rome, is that what you're saying?" he repeated. "You would be with me again if I made this sacrifice?"

"I never said that. I'm just saying —"

"Then what the fuck are you saying, Rome? Because I need to know this goddamn information." He came back to me, standing in front of me with his arms by his sides. The elevator finally came to a stop, and the doors opened, revealing an empty lobby.

My body responded to his like it usually did, making my stomach ache and my heart weep with longing. "It doesn't matter what I said. You aren't going to change. You made that perfectly clear. And I'm not gonna change either. I want marriage, kids, a goddamn white picket fence and to be so madly in love that people want to vomit when they look at us." I didn't care if he judged me for being a hopeless romantic. I didn't care if he thought I was like every other woman in the world who wanted a Prince Charming.

His hand moved to my cheek, this thumb brushing over my bottom lip. His eyes were glued to mine, his gentleness coming out of nowhere. "Would you want all of that with me?"

The air left my lungs at the question. "I told you I loved you, didn't I?"

His thumb paused at the corner of my mouth. "Then your answer is yes. You would give me another chance?"

"Would you really give up your...preferences?" I knew what his answer would be before he gave it.

He lowered his hand and stepped back, not answering the question at all. The elevator doors began to close, so he held them open with his arm. He gave me a nod, telling me to walk out first.

I hid my disappointment when he didn't reconsider. I wanted to burst into tears because I felt rejected all over again. He wanted me, but not enough. He'd rather have a new woman in his life, one who would take a whip and like it. It was better than trying to make it work with me, to having vanilla sex every night with a woman who actually cared about him. I headed straight for the doors with my head held high. He'd just wounded me all over again, but like last time, I wouldn't let it show.

I refused to let it show.

"Rome." Calloway caught up to me on the sidewalk, his hand moving to my upper arm.

I twisted out of the hold. "Don't touch me."

He pulled his hand away, the hurt in his eyes.

"Good night, Calloway." I veered to the left even though it was in the opposite direction of my apartment. If I had to loop around on a different block, that was still better than moving around him. Without turning around, I could feel his gaze pierce into my back. He watched me walk out of his life once again.

14

CALLOWAY

"When are you going to snap out of this?" Jackson walked into my office, catching me off guard even though he never bothered to be quiet when he entered without knocking. "When you were with her, you were boring. But now, you're *super* boring."

I ignored his comment—like all the others. "I hired some new dancers. They'll start this Friday night. I think it'll shake up the entertainment."

"Dancers?"

"In cages with gas masks."

"Ooh...maybe you're a little less boring."

I cracked a smile—a fake one. "I've got a new vendor who asked me to put his vodka in our bar. Tastes pretty good, so I thought I would give it a try."

"New booze. That's always nice." He fell into the

armchair and interlocked his fingers behind his neck. "So...I talked to Isabella today."

"I sincerely hope you didn't tell her I was available. It's one thing to reject a woman when I have a partner. But it's just cruel to reject her when I'm free."

"Reject her?" He moved his arms to the armrests. "I assumed you two would pick up where you left off."

"No." I didn't do back-to-backs. Wasn't my thing. I'd had a long relationship with Isabella. It had its ups and downs, but it was over. I couldn't put it more simply than that. "I'm not looking for anything right now."

"Why? They say you should get back on the horse, right?"

"There's only one horse I want to get on."

He rolled his eyes. "Still brooding over her, huh?"

I pressed my fingertips together, what I usually did when I sat at my desk and busied myself with depressing thoughts. "Yes, Jackson. Just as devastated as I was last week."

He knew I wasn't in the mood for his taunts. "Why don't you just make it work with her?"

"She doesn't want to be my sub."

"Then don't make her. Just be her boyfriend. If you're this miserable anyway, what's the harm in making the compromise?"

"I can't do that." I shook my head, my jaw clenched. It wasn't in my nature. I was surprised our vanilla sex had lasted as long as it did. If it were any other woman, I would have lost interest a long time ago.

"Then how about you meet each other halfway?"

"There is no halfway, Jackson. Maybe you need to get your IQ checked."

"What if she's not your sub, and you aren't her boyfriend?"

I raised an eyebrow. "Then what are we?"

"Whatever you were before. But you do your Dom stuff without her around."

"So, you want me to cheat on her?"

"I never said cheat." He held up a finger like he was correcting me. "A Dom needs control. He needs to be obeyed from beginning to end. You could get what you need from a different arrangement so you don't feel frustrated with Rome. I'm sure Isabella wouldn't mind being bossed around again—even if she doesn't get sex."

The idea had never crossed my mind. But it didn't sound so bad. I would love to have someone submit to me again, to not even look me in the eye unless I gave her explicit permission. Rome was far too strong to bow to me—even though I loved that about her. It was a contradiction, one that didn't make any sense.

"What do you think?" Jackson asked. "It's a win-win."

"I doubt Rome would be happy about it."

"Who said she has to know? You didn't tell her about Ruin for six months."

I still didn't like the idea. "Thanks for trying to help, but I can't do that."

He shrugged and leaned back into the chair. "Then, what? How long are you going to mope around for?"

Probably forever. "I don't know…"

"What is it about this chick? You've been exactly the same guy forever. But the second she came into your life, you changed. And even though she's gone, it doesn't seem like you'll go back to who you were. She changed you permanently."

She did. Now I had a permanent scar on my skin. My lips would always contain her kiss. My hands would always carry her smell. The backs of my eyes were carved with the image of her face. She stole so much from me, and she didn't even know it. "Yeah, I think she did."

"And you really can't make it work with her?" he asked incredulously. "If she's the one…she's the one."

I cared about Rome a great deal, but I wouldn't go that far. A connection existed between us, and she had my undying commitment. I felt differently toward her than I did with other women. She was special, there was no doubt about it. But I couldn't give her marriage and kids. I couldn't give her a house and a picket fence —not when I wanted whips and chains. "She's not the one. There is no *the one*."

Jackson finally gave up. "If it's really over, you need to move on."

"I know."

"The sooner, the better. You know I hate your guts, but I also hate seeing you like this." He left the chair then rapped his knuckles against my desk, like that was some form of affection. Then he walked out and left me alone with my thoughts.

My thoughts about Rome.

I went to see my mom that Saturday.

Everything was exactly the same. The Harry Potter book was tucked under my arm, it was a sunny day, so she would be sitting on the balcony, and I wore the scarf she knitted for me—the one she wouldn't remember giving me.

But this time, Rome wasn't with me.

I didn't feel nearly as much pain for my mother when Rome was there to share the burden. She made things much easier, even pleasant. I still didn't know what possessed me to bring Rome in the first place. It was an impulse decision, an action without motivation.

As always, the nurse introduced me to my mother. "Calloway is here to see you. He's from Humanitarians United, and he's going to read to you." She patted my mother on the back then gave us some privacy.

I sat down in the chair, feeling strange wearing a scarf. The pressure around my neck was unusual, but I wore it anyway because it was so special to me. She wouldn't remember the hours it took to make it. She wouldn't remember giving it to me. But that didn't matter.

She stared at me in silence, her eyes taking in my features like she'd never seen me before.

As always, it was a stab to the heart. "I brought the first Harry Potter book. I've never read it, so I thought we could enjoy it together."

Her eyes moved to my scarf. "That's lovely…" She lifted her hand and pointed several of her fingers in my direction. "The colors look nice on you. The blue brings out your eyes."

I held her gaze and nodded. "Thank you. Someone special made it for me." I opened the book to the first page. Just when I began to read, she interrupted me.

"I feel like I know you from somewhere…"

My eyes remained glued to the book, but I felt my hands shake. She'd never said anything like that, not once in all these years. Her mind had slipped away a long time ago, and she'd never given us any hope for improvement.

I met her gaze once again, seeing the blue eyes that were identical to my own.

She continued to study me, looking at me like a painting on the wall of an art gallery. She took in my features, committing them to a memory that she wouldn't maintain. If she remembered that I was her oldest son, it would be a miracle.

I shouldn't get my hopes up.

"You were here before…with a woman."

I released the book, and it slid down my knees and hit the floor. I didn't bother picking it up because I was in shock. Every night when my mother went to sleep, all the events, conversations, and activities of that day were wiped clean. She woke up the following morning without a single recollection. The nurses had to explain that she lived in a nursing home now because it was the best place for her. "Yes…"

"Where is she?"

Rome wasn't by my side because she wasn't in my life anymore. But I didn't think I had the strength to say that out loud. "She couldn't make it today…"

"Oh…" My mom didn't hide her disappointment. "Lovely girl. I enjoyed the sound of her voice."

She remembered Rome more than she remembered me. It made me both happy and fiercely depressed.

"Something about her," she whispered. "I enjoyed her company."

"Do you enjoy mine?" I don't know what possessed me to say that. It just came out, my frustration obvious. I lived a life of cold cruelty, having no emotions. I told myself I didn't need anyone because I didn't. But I came here every Saturday because I was missing something. I was a grown man who'd been taking care of himself for decades. But I would always have a spot in my heart for my mother, the woman who nurtured me into adulthood. The only good childhood memories I had came from her.

She watched me with pursed lips and a confused gaze. "Of course. Is this woman your wife?"

"No." Even when my mom didn't recognize me, she still pushed me to get married.

"Are you hoping to make her your wife?"

"No."

Her lips fell into a frown. "That's a shame. The woman is perfect."

"You don't know her." My mom didn't even know what she'd had for dinner last night.

"But I can tell. And I could have sworn she meant something to you. I remember the way you looked at her…"

I grabbed the book off the floor and placed it on the chair beside me. Why did Rome, a complete stranger, elicit so much emotion from my mother that she could actually remember her? But my mom didn't recognize her own son? I had to admit, I was a little jealous. "She does mean a lot to me. But we want different things."

"What kind of different things?"

"She wants marriage and kids. And I want to be alone forever." It was a simple reasoning. I didn't need to explain to my mother that I was a creature of the underworld, just like my father, the man she despised.

"Who wants to be alone forever?" She cocked her head as she stared me down, her authoritative tone emerging like it had never left. I remembered the way she straightened me out when she caught me feeling up a girl when I was thirteen. Even though I was a teenager, she whipped my ass with a belt. "I live in a nursing home with no friends or family. Being alone is overrated."

"You aren't alone," I whispered. "I'm here."

"Yes, but it's not the same. Do you want to end up like this?"

The idea of losing my memory, of forgetting about

all the people I cared about and who cared about me, was devastating. To live out the rest of my life without someone to remind me of the beautiful life I had once before seemed harsh. That was a whole new kind of alone, to be trapped in your own mind with no way out.

"Calloway." She said my name the same way she had a million times in my childhood. "All handsome young men want to sow their seeds forever. I was young once. I understand. But there will only be one amazing woman to walk into your life. There's never two—only one. So, you can give up your ways and choose a life of forever happiness. Or you can keep sowing your seeds, watch her end up with someone else, and at the end of your lonely life, you can find yourself like me—sitting on a balcony all alone."

She was giving me a lecture—just like she used to. I couldn't help but smile at the irony. I hadn't had an experience like this with my mother in decades. It was refreshing to experience a normal familial relationship again.

"That's my best advice, Calloway. I hope you take it seriously."

I nodded. "I will, Theresa."

She eyed the book beside me. "If you're willing to read, I'm willing to listen."

"Of course." I opened the book again, watching her

lean her head back and look across the lawn and the gardens at the edge of the property. The sun fell on her face, highlighting her elegant features. She still wore the red lipstick that sometimes smeared her front teeth. The gold earrings in her lobes were a pair her mother gave her for her sixteenth birthday. Her wedding ring was missing from her left hand, either lost or tossed. My eyes moved to the first sentence, and I began to read.

15

ROME

I grabbed the mail from the lobby then headed to my floor. It was mostly bills, and a big fat one for my student loans. But I didn't feel a twinge of sadness when I looked at the amount I still owed, along with my ridiculous interest that just seemed to only get bigger. My depression over Calloway was constantly at the forefront.

I was pissed at him, but damn, I really missed him.

He'd walked away from me for the second time, unwilling to give me what I wanted. I sure as hell wasn't going to cave, so we were going to be at this stalemate forever. Soon, he would find the kind of woman he wanted and would forget about me.

I was sure he had women lined up already. Even if they weren't completely involved in the lifestyle, they would put up with it for a chance to be with Calloway.

He was all man, powerful and masculine, with a strong body that made him look like a Navy SEAL. He had the most gorgeous eyes and the sexiest kiss. Sometimes, when I thought about how amazing he was, I didn't care about all the horrible things he wanted to do to me. I wanted him that much.

But then reality kicked in.

I put my key in the door but realized it was already unlocked. The doorknob shifted loosely, like something inside the mechanism was busted. I pushed open the door and assumed Christopher was already home even though he usually hit the gym after work.

I walked inside and set my mail on the table along with my purse.

"Just as beautiful as the last time I saw you."

The words moved along my spine, making me tense with impending doom. Adrenaline spiked, and my heart kicked into overdrive once I recognized the threat. I knew that voice anywhere—because I heard it in my nightmares almost every night.

I looked into the living room and saw Hank sitting on the couch, his fingers interlocked behind his head. He wore a three-piece suit, handsome and formidable. He reeked of unstoppable power.

I was scared.

I wasn't going to lie to myself and say I wasn't. I

was alone in an apartment with this man, and his intentions were quite clear. My hands shook slightly, but I forced them to remain still. In a moment like this, it was essential to appear calm and confident, to make him think I was a stronger opponent than I truly was.

The island separated me from the rest of the kitchen. I discreetly glanced at the knives in the knife block on the counter, but I realized they were all missing.

He'd swept the apartment clean.

Fuck.

"And you're just as disgusting as the last time I saw you." I placed my hand on my hip and turned to face him, diffusing the obvious hostility as much as possible. He'd planned this meticulously, making sure I had no weapon to fight him off. I doubted he wanted to kill me—but I knew he wanted to do something far worse.

He grinned like he enjoyed the banter. "So fiery but so innocent. I love it."

I wasn't innocent anymore. Calloway had stripped me of my purity.

The thought of Calloway made me wince in pain. If he were here, this wouldn't be happening. Calloway would protect me from Hank with just a single look. I didn't need a man to fight my battles, but I was scared and vulnerable. So having him around would have been extremely helpful.

I couldn't let Hank succeed because I didn't deserve this. But also because I didn't want to break Calloway's heart. If he knew what Hank was about to do to me, he would throw himself off the Empire State Building.

I had to make sure I didn't lose—for both of us.

"Is there something I can help you with, Hank? Perhaps setting up your Tinder account so you can find a date?"

He chuckled then rose to his feet, towering above me with over six feet of strength. "Why find another woman when I have you?"

The moment he stood up, my body tensed again. The fight-or-flight instinct was kicking in. As he moved closer to me, I knew I needed an escape route. He was too strong for me to fight off alone. The best thing would be to sprint into the hallway and scream for help. Someone was bound to hear me.

He slowly came closer to me, his eyes darkening as he looked me up and down in my tight dress. "You're looking damn fine today."

I wanted to spit in disgust. I couldn't believe I'd ever kissed this man, that I ever got on my knees for him. He pretended to be an angel that wanted to help me, but he turned into the devil instead. Men who preyed on vulnerable people were scum to me — worse than scum.

I had to do something. And I had to do it now. "You know, I find it — " I sprinted to the door without looking back, hoping he was absorbed in my words to give me a one-second head start.

"You think you're getting away?" His loud voice followed me out the door.

I kicked my shoes off and sprinted as hard as I could, but with lightning speed, he caught up to me.

He grabbed me by the back of the neck and slammed me into the wall, knocking my head against the solid material. "You'll never get away from me, Rome. When will you understand that?" He covered my mouth with his hand so I couldn't scream.

I saw stars, and the world spun. His arm hooked around my waist, and he used his strength to press me into the wall.

"I've earned the right to fuck you," he hissed into my ear. "You teased me for so long, after everything I did for you. It's gonna happen, bitch. Might as well accept that." He yanked me down the hall and left my heels behind.

I couldn't let this happen.

Once he got me back into the apartment, the game was over.

I ignored the blinding pain from my skull and mustered up energy from every inch. of my body. I threw my head back hard, striking him right in the nose. It probably hurt me more than it hurt him. But pain was better than being pinned onto my bed while he fucked me like he owned me.

I grabbed his arm and twisted it behind his neck. I kicked his knee, forcing him to fall to the ground. I grabbed his head and slammed my knee into his face, this time breaking his nose and making blood stream everywhere. "I've earned the right to kick your ass, bitch-face." I shoved him into the wall just the way he'd shoved me, making sure his skull collided with the molding along the side.

He fell to the ground but didn't lose consciousness. He rolled out of the way, getting blood everywhere. It soaked into the carpets and streaked along the white walls. He managed to grab my foot then twisted it painfully, forcing me to fall to my knee with a painful thud.

Instinctively, I threw my elbow down onto his wrist, making him cry out in pain. He immediately released my foot and pulled his hand into his chest, cradling it like it might be broken.

The elevator at the very end of the hallway beeped as it approached the floor. The doors were about to open, and my neighbors were going to save me. They would take one look at Hank, me, and the blood then call the cops.

Hank gave me a terrifying look. "This isn't over, baby." He got to his feet and ran to the stairwell at the opposite end of the hall just as the doors opened.

I would have chased him, but I couldn't move. I was exhausted from the battle and in immense pain. My foot hurt, but I was certain it wasn't broken. My head throbbed with the worst migraine of my life.

"Rome!" Christopher sprinted down the hallway until he came to my side on the floor. He spotted the blood and the bruises on my face, and without asking any questions, he figured out exactly what had happened. "Let's get you to the hospital. I'll call the police on the way. Can you walk?"

"Yes..." I got to my feet and felt dizzy. But I refused to show weakness even though I wasn't sure why. I needed to walk away from the battle as the victor, not the defeated.

Christopher scooped me into his arms and carried me back to the elevator, leaving my shoes in the hallway. Somehow, he managed to pull out his phone and press it between his neck and shoulder. The elevator carried us to the lobby as he made the call. The operator's voice came on the line. "9-1-1. What's your emergency?"

"I'm calling to report an assault."

***

After a day at the hospital, I learned I had a concussion, bruised ribs, and a lightly sprained foot.

But other than that, I was in good shape.

It could have been worse, so I counted it as a blessing.

Christopher got the police involved even though I knew it wouldn't go anywhere. They investigated the apartment and the scene in the hallway, but once Christopher accused Hank of being the culprit, they created other suspects, criminals and felons that lived within a two-mile radius. Apparently, Hank had a solid alibi—he was taking counsel with a client. His client, two cops, and even a judge insisted he was with them at the time of the crime.

So he was immediately ruled out.

Christopher was pissed, but I wasn't surprised. How do you take down the face of New York City? How do you get him to pay for his crimes when everyone covers for him all the time? He had too much leverage and too much power over far too many people.

Christopher called in sick for me, saying I had a nasty case of the flu. I was grateful he didn't give them the truth, because if Calloway knew, it would be bad news.

I was in the hospital for three days before they released me. I was good as new, with the exception of my foot. Sometimes it hurt to walk on it, but only slightly. I knew it would get better as time went by. It was just a matter of being patient.

Christopher and I hadn't talked much over the past few days. He was too angry to say a single word. I could tell he was about to explode at any moment, and then his words would rain down on me like fire.

The door to the apartment had been fixed, and the hallway was as good as new. One of the neighbors moved out after they heard about the attack, obviously too afraid to live anywhere near me.

Not that I blamed them.

It felt good to be home again, but it also didn't feel like home anymore. Hank had sat on one of the couches and hid all our knives under the sink. Just the fact that he was ever there made it seem less cozy.

Christopher grabbed a beer from the fridge and sat on the couch, looking just as angry as he did three days earlier.

"Thanks for taking care of me…" There were no

words to express my gratitude. He took time off work to stay at the hospital with me. When he asked if he could call Calloway, I said no. And he'd respected my wishes.

He drank his beer and said nothing.

I sat on the other couch, knowing the conversation was coming. We had to talk about this. It was obvious Christopher was working up to it, his jaw clenching and unclenching. "The cops aren't going to do anything about this because they're absolutely worthless. So, we need to do something."

"I'm out of ideas," I whispered. "I've taken him on countless times in the past. I know I can hold my own in a fight—"

"You're missing the point, Rome. You shouldn't have to live like this." He slammed his beer down, making the table shake with force.

"I know…"

"No woman should have to feel like prey every single day of her life. How can the justice system fail you like this?"

"It's not the justice system's fault. It's Hank's."

"Same difference," he snapped. "The guy owns all the cops in this city. It's fucking ridiculous."

"I told you, Christopher."

He shook his head and looked at the ground. "Unbelievable…"

"I know." I felt terrible for putting him through this, for stressing him out with worry over me. "I'm sorry."

"Don't you dare apologize, Rome," he whispered. "It's not your fault."

I was still sorry anyway. I was sorry I took Hank's help on the street that afternoon. I was sorry I got Christopher mixed up in this, making him so upset that he wanted to break everything inside the apartment. Believe me, if I could've made Hank go away, I would've. But this was just a game to him. He would keep playing until he won.

"I think we should tell Calloway." He interlocked his fingers, his head bowed toward the floor.

"What?" Calloway was the last person we should involve. "I'm not seeing him anymore, Christopher."

"I know you aren't. But I think he could help us."

"Help us how?" By murdering Hank? I could do that just fine on my own.

"Calloway is powerful. He's done more for this city than everyone else combined. His rehabilitation program has put more ex-cons to work and kept them out of jail than any other federal program. Every judge, lawyer, and city official knows exactly who he is. If it's Calloway's word against Hank's, I think Calloway stands a fair chance. And even if he doesn't, Hank would be afraid of him."

"Why?"

"Because he's huge. His arms are the size of my head."

I wouldn't admit to anyone that Calloway made me feel safe. Whenever I stayed at his place, I felt untouchable. "I'm not bringing him into this. He's not my boyfriend anymore. I'm sorry that you're involved with this at all. I can just move out — "

"Shut up, Rome," he snapped. "I'm not trying to hand you off to someone else because I can't handle it. I just think getting him involved would help. He might have an approach we aren't considering. This guy knows a lot of people — including those from the underworld."

If I told Calloway what was going on, he would explode. He would destroy everything he built by doing something stupid. I wouldn't be surprised if he grabbed my things and forced me to move in with him, like a bear dragging his cub back to the den. "No."

"Why?" he hissed. "Give me one good reason why."

"He's. Not. My. Boyfriend." Calloway was just a man from my past. We worked together, but I wouldn't consider us to be friends. My problems weren't his problems—not anymore. "Christopher, we'll figure this out on our own."

"Like hell, we will," he hissed. "We have no defense against this guy. Even if I got a gun, I couldn't use it against him. I would be thrown in jail for murder instead of hailed as a hero for saving my sister."

"I know...but he'll lose interest eventually."

"After he rapes you," he hissed. "And no, we aren't letting him get his way. He's a fucking brat that never learned a single lesson in his life. He's scum."

"He can't do this forever. One day, he'll get married and have kids."

"Who knows how long that will take. In the meantime, we'll walk on eggshells for the rest of our lives?" He shook his head, rage brewing in his eyes. "I'm not living like that, Rome. And you aren't either."

Christopher had every right to be frustrated, so I let him vent all his anger. "We'll figure it out one way or another. But I don't think getting Calloway involved is the answer. It's you and me. We can do this."

He dragged his hands down his face in anger.

"Christopher?"

"What?"

"We're in this together, okay?"

He finally nodded, releasing a sigh. "Yeah. Just you and me."

My bruises were pretty much gone, and the blue color could easily be hidden with makeup. My foot was better, but I wasn't able to wear heels just yet. I could wear flats around the office for a day or so without anyone asking questions.

I lay in bed but couldn't sleep despite how exhausted I was. At the hospital, I slept like a baby because I knew Hank couldn't get to me. But now that I was in the apartment, a place he'd already broken in to, I didn't feel safe. Christopher slept across the hall, his bedroom door opened so he could hear the sounds of the apartment, but that still didn't chase away the fear.

My phone vibrated on my nightstand then the screen lit up with a message.

From Calloway.

I know I should leave you alone, but I'm worried. My assistant told me you've had the flu for three days. I just wanted to check on you.

My eyes burned with tears at the words, wishing I could tell him everything that had happened to me lately. I missed sharing my life with him, telling him about the ups and downs. I didn't just miss him as my lover, but as my friend. *The worst is over. I'll be back in the office tomorrow.*

I'm glad to hear that. You must have caught it when we were under the bridge earlier this week.

I remembered that day better than any other. He somehow broke my heart for the second time. *Yeah. Maybe.*

I'll let you go to sleep.

I didn't want to go to sleep, not in this tainted apartment. I wanted to lie against his hard chest, feeling at peace because no one could reach me. I wanted those strong arms to wrap around my body. I wanted him to look me in the eye as he made love to me. Tears bubbled until they formed drops and slid down my cheeks. Letting out the grief didn't make me feel better—just worse. *Good night.*

Good night, sweetheart.

16

CALLOWAY

I caught a glimpse of Rome the next day at work.

I walked into the break room just as she was leaving. My arm brushed against her shoulder, sending chills down my spine despite the juvenile touch. I got a whiff of her scent, beautiful and seductive. I suddenly pictured her underneath me, her mouth forming that sexy O as she came all over my dick.

Fuck, I missed her.

I missed fucking her.

I spent the rest of the day in my office, grateful she was back on her feet and moving around. She didn't seem sick anymore, but then again, I was only in her presence for two seconds.

Normally, my driver took me home from work, but I'd been walking lately. The cold air and the sound of traffic seemed to minimize the pain in my chest. I had nowhere to be, so I wasn't exactly in a hurry.

When I walked up to my front door, Christopher was standing there. His hands were in his pockets as he leaned against the wall beside my door, his ankles crossed. His hair was untidy like he hadn't bothered doing it that morning. His shoes weren't as polished as usual either. "Didn't expect to see you again." I walked up the stoop until we were eye to eye. "Hope everything is okay."

"No." He flashed me a venomous look. "Everything is not fucking okay."

"I haven't slept with anyone." Did he come over here to tell me off again? I'd already admitted my crimes and apologized for them. It was time to move on.

"No, not about that. Let's go inside."

I ignored the way he invited himself into my house. I got the door unlocked and we entered. I dropped my jacket on the coatrack and watched him do the same. "You want a beer—"

"No." He locked the door behind him even though it was unnecessary. I lived in a great neighborhood. No one was going to break in and loot the place—at least if they weren't stupid. "Rome doesn't know I'm here, and I've got to make this quick."

At the mention of her name, he had my full

attention. "What's up?" I hoped he would try to put us back together, to tell me Rome missed me and I just needed to fight harder for her. The longer I went without kissing her or touching her, the more insane I became. I was slowly losing my mind, missing that woman in my bed.

"It's a fucking nightmare, man. I need your help."

All my hope deflated. "What is it?"

"You remember that ex-boyfriend of hers?"

I didn't like where this was going. I was already pissed—instantly. "Yes."

"She told you what happened with him, right?"

Both of my hands formed fists. "Yes."

"Well, what she didn't tell you is he's been stalking her for a while now."

Stalking her? What the fuck? "What the hell did you just say?"

"You're mad now..." He chuckled like this was somehow funny. "The reason why I asked you to give her a job at your office is because Hank went to her office a few months ago and harassed her. Luckily, I was there, so that scared him off, but apparently, he'd done it a few times."

What. The. Fuck.

I'm gonna kill him.

I don't need a gun or a knife. My hands would do.

I couldn't speak because I was too angry. And that was a first.

Christopher continued when I remained silent. "She moved in with me, which I think was a great decision because of Hank. But a few days ago, he broke in to our apartment and ambushed her when she came home. They fought in the hallway. She broke his nose and wrist but took some damage herself. She wasn't really sick. She was in the hospital."

Now I couldn't breathe.

He'd touched her.

He'd placed his hands on her.

Hurt her.

I stepped back slowly until the backs of my legs hit the couch. I fell with a thump onto the cushion, my heart beating so fast it actually hurt. I couldn't catch my breath. So much adrenaline. So much fucking pain.

Christopher told me about his attempt with the cops and how it didn't go anywhere. This man was too powerful as the DA for New York City. The guy was pretty much untouchable.

Until now.

Christopher watched me closely. "You haven't said anything in about five minutes. Are you okay?"

I processed so much shit in minutes, and it took my

brain a second to catch up. When I found my strength, I stood up again. "I can't believe she didn't tell me..."

"Since you aren't seeing each other anymore—"

"I was seeing her the first two times he assaulted her." I was yelling at Christopher even though he hadn't done anything wrong. "I'll take care of this."

"What are you going to do?"

"I don't know yet. But this problem is officially gone." I stormed out of my own house and left Christopher behind, not giving a damn if he stayed or went. I didn't even grab my phone or my keys.

And I ran all the way to Rome.

"Open the fucking door!" I slammed my fists into the wood like I was playing the drums. I kept knocking, bruising my knuckles without feeling even a hint of pain. "Rome, do as I say, or I'm gonna break it down."

When she finally opened the door, she wore a resigned expression on her face. "I can't believe he told you..."

I slammed the door so hard behind me the walls shook. "And I can't believe you didn't tell me." I rushed her, forcing her back to hit the kitchen counter. My hands gripped the counter on either side of her as I got in her face, feeling so much anger—most of it directed at her. "You have a lot of fucking nerve, you know that?"

"What?" Clearly, that was the last thing she'd expected me to say.

"You left me because of my skeletons. But you have bigger ones. This asshole has been stalking you for months, and you didn't run it by me? You didn't think that was important information that I needed to know?" My nose pressed against hers as I continued to yell. "That my girlfriend could have been raped or taken, and I wouldn't have had a clue about it. Fuck you, Rome." I finally stepped back, my hands curling into fists.

Shocked, she stared at me with a pale face.

"Pack your shit. Now."

"Whoa, what?" She couldn't keep up with my thoughts.

I walked back to her, returning my hands to where they had been. "Pack. Your. Shit. You're living with me until we get this taken care of."

"I am not—"

"You wanna fight me?" I threatened. "Fine. But you're gonna lose, Rome. You're gonna lose so fucking hard." My eyes were wide open, and my hands were shaking. "Do as I say, or I'll make you. What's it gonna be?"

Normally Rome would fight me tooth and nail. But she must have known I'd reached my boiling point. I was so insane with rage I couldn't think straight anymore. Or she was really that scared, too afraid to stay in her own apartment because that psychopath could come back at any moment. "Give me a minute to pack…"

I finally stepped back after she was cooperating. I crossed my arms over my chest and stared her down. "Hurry your ass up. I don't want you in this apartment a moment longer than necessary."

The ride back to my place was saturated with intensity.

My hand was still tight in a fist on my thigh, my knuckles white and about to snap. I kept my eyes glued out the window, not looking at Rome or getting too close to her. I was so angry with her I didn't know what to do with myself. I wanted to strangle her, suffocate her. The betrayal was so searing I couldn't think straight.

She didn't make the mistake of uttering a single word. I didn't give a damn if my driver overheard our entire conversation, but to save herself some embarrassment, she was smart to stay quiet.

We arrived back at the house, and to my surprise, Christopher was still there.

"I didn't know if you were coming back...didn't have a clue how to—" He stopped talking when he saw Rome pulling her suitcase behind her into the house. He eyed her before he turned back to me, silently asking for an explanation.

"She's living with me now." I pointed to the door.

Christopher looked at Rome. "What's going on—"

"We'll talk about it later. But for now, I need to be alone with Rome." I only kept my temper in check because he was kind enough to tell me the truth. But make no mistake, I was on the verge of screaming.

This time, Christopher did as I commanded. He walked out and shut the door, leaving Rome alone with me. Honestly, I wasn't sure if that was a wise thing to do.

Once the door was shut and we were alone together, the silence was deafening. It was so quiet I could hear the blood pounding behind my ears. When I tightened my fists, I could hear the slight crack of my knuckles.

Rome stood beside her suitcase, her arms tight around her waist. It was the first time I'd seen her lose her confidence. She appeared apologetic, knowing she was guilty for what she had done. She didn't hold her head high with elegance, with the respect of a queen.

I asked the biggest question on my mind. "Why didn't you tell me?"

"You know why."

"I really don't." I kept my voice low, but the threat in my tone never faded away. "And you're going to tell me."

"Because I knew you would do something stupid — like murder him."

"That doesn't sound stupid at all — quite the opposite." I wanted this man's body inside a dumpster on 12th Street, rotting away and stinking up the alley. I wanted his corpse to be cut into small pieces, perfect for feeding fish in the harbor.

"He's a very powerful man — "

"And you think I'm not?" I was an opponent that never lost a battle.

"You've worked really hard to build this life. I didn't want to tear you down with this."

"Tear me down?"

"He can make your life a nightmare, Calloway. Christopher has tried intervening, but I know Hank would take his license away, get him fired, and strip away all of his accomplishments. I couldn't let that happen to him. And I'm not gonna let that happen to you."

"I'd like to see him try." I closed the space between us, cornering Rome against the wall. "This is how this is going to work. You live here with me now. I'll take you to work every day and anywhere else you want to go. But you stay in my sight at all times. Got it?"

She wanted to argue. It was obvious by the darkness in her eyes. Her lips pressed tightly together like she was trying to swallow the argument.

"I didn't hear you." I pressed my face closer to hers.

"I think it's a little extreme—"

I grabbed her by the neck, unable to control my temper. "Wrong answer. This guy broke in to your apartment and messed you up. If anything, it's not extreme enough. Now, you will do as I say. Got it?"

She didn't push my hand away, but her eyes broke contact with mine. She was overpowered and outsmarted. She knew she was in the wrong for letting things get so bad without my help. "Okay."

I finally dropped my hold and grabbed her suitcase, prepared to take her things to one of the spare bedrooms. "You're staying with me until I figure this out. You are not to go anywhere without telling me. You are not to do anything without me knowing about it. So, forget about going on any dates or spending time with friends."

I sat in the living room while she remained upstairs in her bedroom. I needed some time alone, to meditate and release all the anger bubbling inside me. I was so angry at Rome for not telling me, for needing my protection but never asking for it. But I was even more livid with the man responsible for this situation, the one who was stupid enough to think he could haunt my girl and get away with it.

I needed to come up with a plan to get rid of him once and for all.

As much as I would have liked to murder Hank, that wouldn't work. He was too well-known by everyone in the city to just vanish. I had to learn more about this guy and figure out the best way to dissolve him, to kill his obsession with Rome.

Rome's footsteps broke my train of thought. She descended the stairs and entered the living room, still in the same clothes she wore earlier. She'd been in her bedroom for hours, probably waiting until my wrath dispersed.

Not gonna happen.

She fell onto the chair beside me, her dress moving up above her knee. She pulled her hair over one shoulder, revealing her slender and beautiful neck. The smell of vanilla immediately struck me, bringing with it memories of our nights together.

I was still angry with her, and I suspected I would always be angry with her.

"What now?" she whispered.

"I'm thinking."

"You can't kill him, Calloway. Neither one of us would be able to get away with it."

The fact that she'd already considered murder made me feel a little better. "I know."

"This guy is a nightmare. I'm not sure how to get rid of him."

"Trust me, I'll figure it out." I wasn't going to let Rome be a target any longer. Where she went, I went. And if he came after her, he would have to deal with me. Now that she was beside me and our conversation was relatively calm, I turned my chin and looked at her, seeing her green eyes dark and dormant. I could see the faint bruising around her left eye, the place where Hank had struck her. The image of her fighting him off so she wouldn't be raped killed me inside. Rome lived a selfless life of helping others. Of all people, she deserved this the least.

My hand moved to her cheek then into her hair while my lips kissed the faded bruise. Her skin felt cold to my lips, not warm from the fire like I was used to. My arm circled her waist, and I kissed her forehead, touching her for the first time in a month. At the first contact, my hands shook. I missed this affection more than I'd realized—and I already knew I missed it a great deal. "Everything will be alright. You don't need to be scared anymore."

Normally, she would argue and say she wasn't afraid of anything. She would tell me she didn't need me —or anyone else. Her tough persona would come out, her fists raised. But she didn't do that this time. That was all the confirmation I needed. She had finally reached the end of the road. She was exhausted by the constant battle, knowing Hank would catch her off guard over and over.

My hand moved down her back, gently massaging her. "I won't let anything happen to you." I wasn't letting her out of my sight until I knew Hank was really gone. I was excited that I'd get to spend more time with her, but I also loathed the idea because nothing had changed between us. She wanted romance, and I wanted whips and chains. She wanted to get married, and I wanted to be single until my last breath.

My conversation with my mother came back to me,

and I pictured myself sitting on that balcony instead of her. No one would come to visit me, not even Jackson. I would have no children to remember me by, to come and read to me. There would be no wife to hold my hand and comfort me, even though she'd know I didn't recognize her.

But those depressing images didn't get to me. It was the fact that my life had nothing to show for it. If I lived a meaningless life, I would have a meaningless death. My need for control was irrelevant because I had no control over my own destiny.

"Calloway?"

Rome's beautiful voice brought me back to the conversation.

"You slipped away…" She still remembered all my expressions like we hadn't been apart.

"Just…" I didn't know how to form my answer because I wasn't entirely sure what I was thinking about. I'd never felt so confused. Before Rome walked into my life, I never thought about these things. But now, I was filled with doubt. "Nothing."

Rome didn't press her curiosity.

"I'm glad you're alright." I turned my attention back to her, my fingers worshiping her soft hair. I wanted to erase what had happened to her, to end Hank before he had the chance to even look at her ever again. This woman meant the world to me. When she hurt, I hurt. "If anything worse happened to you..." I couldn't finish the sentence because it was too difficult. Just the suggestion of Hank overpowering her made me sick to my stomach.

"But nothing did." Her slender fingers wrapped around my wrist, still cold. "That's all that matters."

I stared at her lips and ached to kiss her, to feel those soft lips against my mouth. I wanted to roll around on my sheets while I was buried deep inside her. I wanted to feel that connection with her, that powerful voltage that always healed all my aches and wounds. But she and I were still worlds apart.

Rome must have felt the connection too because she excused herself. "I should go to bed. It'll be nice to get some sleep tonight. Haven't been able to close my eyes for a few days..."

Probably because she was terrified that asshole would come back to the apartment. "Good night." I unwillingly released her and watched her walk up the stairs until she was gone from my sight.

When I was alone, I lay back and stared at the blank TV. The woman of my dreams shared the house with me, her bedroom just down the hall from mine. Would I be able to stay in my own room and not slip under the sheets with her? I didn't have a lot of self-control — not when it came to Rome.

I tried to get some sleep, but it was pointless. I stared at the ceiling in the dark, my hand resting on my chest. I hadn't gotten laid in a month, and I knew that messed my cycle up. And I knew it had something to do with the brunette across the hall.

I didn't own a gun, but I didn't need one. If Hank somehow figured out Rome was here, I could take him down with my own fists. I wasn't sure how he would even figure out she was in the house. He'd have to be stalking her like he was staring at her through a microscope.

A gentle knock sounded on my bedroom door before it cracked open.

I sat up in bed automatically, my reflexes taking over.

Rome poked her head inside, wearing one of my old t-shirts. She must have taken it with her when she left. I hadn't seen it around the house in weeks. "Sorry to wake you…"

"I wasn't asleep." I stared her down and waited for an explanation.

"Can I sleep with you?" She asked the question as if it caused her pain to say the words out loud. "I can't sleep—"

"Yes." There was nothing I wanted more than to have this woman in my bed again. She wouldn't be the only one to finally get some sleep. I would too. I pulled down the covers and patted the sheets beside me. "Come here."

She walked to the bed then climbed inside, looking beautiful in my clothes. Her cold body lay beside mine, and she pulled the sheets over herself, surrounded by the warmth my body produced.

The second she was beside me, I grabbed her leg and hooked it over my waist, feeling her smooth skin under my fingertips. My face rested against hers, and the pain immediately stopped. Just having her next to me made me feel better, made me feel some form of joy. My cock was hard, and I knew she could feel it, but that was beyond my control. I was so hard up for her that my dick thickened anytime we were in the same room together.

She cuddled against my chest and sighed deeply, like she was finally relaxing and drifting away. Her hand circled my waist, and her strands tickled my skin at the slightest movement. It felt like we were four months in the past, when the two of us were better together than apart.

I pressed a kiss to her forehead, feeling my thoughts slip away. "Good night, sweetheart."

"Good night, Sexy…"

17

ROME

I hadn't slept that well in four days.

It felt so good.

The second my head hit the pillow as I lay beside Calloway, my lights went out. Knowing I was safe in this castle with the king right beside me, I knew I was untouchable. I could finally let my guard down and get some real sleep.

The next morning, I didn't want to get out of bed. Not because I was too tired, but because I was so comfortable. The sheets smelled like his body soap with a splash of mint, pure Calloway, and they were so soft to the touch. I missed lying in bed every Saturday, touching the strong muscles all over Calloway's body.

When the alarm sounded, Calloway turned it off then sat up in bed. His back was to me as he stretched his arms, his muscles coiling and shifting under his skin as he moved.

I wanted to reach out to touch him, but I kept my hands to myself. "How'd you sleep?"

"Like a rock." He stared straight ahead before he rose to his feet, standing in his boxers. With toned thighs and long legs, he looked like the ultimate definition of what a man should be. "You?"

"Good."

Without another word, he walked into the bathroom and got into the shower.

I expected him to make a move, to get me naked while I was in his bed, but he didn't initiate anything. His cock had been hard. I'd felt it pressed against my hip. But sex didn't seem to be on his mind. He was probably too upset with everything.

I got ready in the other bathroom, and after half an hour, we were both ready to go. Our routine was exactly the same as our old one, and we met at the front door. His driver took us to work, and we entered the building at the same time.

"Maybe I should catch a different elevator?" I asked, not wanting everyone at the office to see us walk in together.

The door opened, and he pointed inside. "No."

"But what if—"

"I don't give a damn." He walked inside and held the door open. "If people think we're fucking, so what? We were fucking, so it's not like they'd be wrong. Now get your ass in here." Calloway stared me down, looking like the devil in a suit.

I didn't enjoy Calloway's authority, but I felt so guilty for not telling him the truth about Hank that I complied. He deserved to be angry and protective. I didn't have any right to take that away from him, so I cooperated. I walked inside the elevator and stood beside him.

He pulled his arm away and let the doors close. Immediately, the elevator rose to the top of the building. Like any other time we were in an enclosed space, I felt electricity prickle my skin. The burn moved through my body, lighting me on fire until I was a brilliant inferno. I wanted to wrap my arms around his neck and kiss him just the way I used to.

I wished he would give me what I wanted. I wished he would change for me.

The door opened, and we walked into the lobby, everyone seeing us arrive at work together. I turned down the hallway to my office, and he went the opposite direction, heading to his massive office against the back wall.

I got to my office and sat down, suddenly missing him more than ever before.

When the workday ended, Calloway appeared in my doorway, looking just as sexy as he did that morning. His suit was still crisp, and his stubble had grown in over the course of the day. His assistant brought me lunch at midday so I wouldn't have to go anywhere, and now that he was here, he would make sure I didn't walk back to his place unaccompanied.

"Are you finished?" he asked, leaning against the doorframe. He crossed his arms over his chest, his watch gleaming in the light.

"Yeah…" I saved the email I was in the middle of writing and put my computer to sleep before I grabbed my purse. I went to his side, knowing our leaving together would confirm everyone's suspicions that we really were together.

But there was nothing I could do to fight it.

We walked out together, two feet in between us the entire time. We made it to the car, and the driver drove us back to Calloway's house a few blocks away. His neighborhood was silent compared to the commotion of the rest of the city.

We walked inside, surrounded by privacy once again. I immediately slipped off my heels and left them by the door, knowing I would wear them the next morning. They hurt my feet every single day, but they were so cute that I couldn't part with them. Plus, I got them for a really great deal.

Calloway undid his tie and left it hanging around his neck, just as he used to do when we came home together. He darted into the kitchen and opened his liquor cabinet, grabbing a bottle of his favorite scotch.

I figured he would start up the habit again.

He pulled a glass from the cabinet just as I grabbed the bottle off the counter. "None of this."

He stared me down with lidded eyes. "We aren't seeing each other anymore. I can do whatever the hell I want." He reached for the bottle.

I stepped back and kept it out of his reach. "You're better than this. I know you are."

"I take a shot to shake the edge off. Doesn't make me an alcoholic."

"But it makes you dependent on it." I unscrewed the cap then held it over the sink, threatening to pour it down the drain. I knew it was aged and expensive, so tossing it would really piss him off. But he didn't need to turn to alcohol every time there was a bump in the road.

He glared viciously at me, his anger palpable. "Don't you dare."

"You can keep it for social occasions."

"We both know I don't have any friends."

"Then maybe you should make some." I put the cap back on then returned it to the cabinet. "I'm gonna trust you not to drink this when I'm not in the room. Can I trust you to do that?" I placed my hands on my hips and watched him, knowing whatever answer he gave would be the truth. He'd lied to me before, but for some reason, I still trusted him.

He eyed the cabinet before he looked at me again. His jaw was clenched with irritation, and he didn't keep the annoyance out of his expression. "Yes." He grabbed the glass sitting on the counter and returned it to the cabinet. He shut the door then leaned against the counter, his arms across his chest.

Now I didn't have to keep an eye on him. "Thank you."

He nodded.

"I'm going to shower…" I turned away from the kitchen, wanting to remove myself from the searing heat between us.

"I'm not done talking to you."

I turned around, annoyed. "You think you can boss

me around now?" I put up with it for a few days, but I was growing tired of it.

"Yes. I'll boss you around as much as I like." His blue eyes were no longer charismatic, but a little frightening. "We need to get to work on Hank. Perhaps you want to do that before you shower. Up to you."

"Get to work on him, how?"

"I need you to tell me everything about him. I want to know where he lives, what he looks like, if his parents are divorced—everything. The more information I have, the easier this will be."

I didn't want to talk about Hank—not now or ever. But there was no way around it. I knew Calloway needed that information, not to kill him, but to destroy him. "Okay."

We had dinner together at the table, dead silent and tense.

Calloway sat across from me, his forearms exposed in his t-shirt. Strong and powerful, he looked like a Roman soldier who could tear down an army all on his own.

"Can I ask you something?" I whispered.

He stopped eating and looked me square in the eye. "You know the answer."

I hoped that was a yes. "How's your mom?"

His eyes flinched like he didn't expect the question. "She's good. I saw her on Saturday."

"She's a sweet woman."

"Yeah..." He spun his fork around his pasta but didn't take a bite. "She remembered you."

I heard the words but struggled to absorb them. "What?"

"She remembered you," he repeated. "She asked where you were." He chuckled, but the laugh was full of pain. "Never remembers me, but somehow, she remembers you..."

"She did? What did she say?"

He set his fork down and pushed his untouched plate away. "That you were lovely."

To my own surprise, my eyes watered. I knew Calloway struggled with his mother's illness. Every time he visited her, it caused him so much pain. She was his mother, but he could never be her son because she didn't remember him.

"She told me to knock off my promiscuous ways and settle down. It's ironic because I can't remember the last time my mother gave me a lecture. It was nice, in a strange way." He leaned back against the chair, one hand resting on the table.

"I don't know what to say…"

"There's nothing to say, Rome. It just seems like you have the same effect on my mother as you do on me… on everyone."

It was a sweet thing to say, and it made my insides tighten with butterflies.

"Sometimes I wonder if she's right…"

"Right about what?"

"Right about you. That I should give up my lifestyle for you." He looked me in the eye as he spoke. "I've been miserable without you. The idea of being with anyone else literally makes me sick. I have the freedom to put someone in chains, but I don't want to…because I only want you. I haven't slept in four weeks because it's not the same without you beside me. Every day, I wonder what you're doing while I'm home alone. I think about you constantly, wondering if you're thinking about me."

"Yes," I whispered. "I am thinking about you — every minute."

His eyes immediately softened. "Sometimes, I think I can give it up. Then other times, I think I can't…"

I wanted him to walk away from Ruin and start over with me. I wanted him to forsake the other half of his soul, the dark shadow that belonged in the night. I wanted him to step into the light with me, so we could spend our lives together as two people who loved each other. But I didn't want to make him do it. He needed to make the decision on his own.

"I can't give you up. But I can't give this up either."

Every time he came to a crossroads, he always chose the life he already knew. He wanted to pick me, but he couldn't bring himself to do it.

"Sometimes, I think I can...but I'm afraid if I turn my back on who I really am, it'll just be worse in the end." He clenched his jaw like he was thinking of a memory from his past, something that angered him.

I was at the same crossroads. I wanted to move on and find a man I could spend the rest of my life with. Someone sweet and compassionate, who would be a great father and husband. But did that really matter when I loved Calloway? When I would always love him?

I loved every aspect about him, even his darker shades. I loved his intensity, his temper. I loved the way he made me feel like a woman when we were in bed together. I loved his fierce need to protect me even though I swore I didn't need it. I loved the way he made me feel small when his thick arm was around my waist. Light and dark, I loved both sides.

Calloway watched me, knowing my mind was working furiously. "Do you still love me?"

My eyes shifted at the question, surprised he even needed to ask. "Always."

His eyes softened again, this time with both pain and longing. "I want to give up everything for you... I just don't think I can."

"I know..."

He leaned forward, his elbows resting on the table. "Meet me in the middle, Rome. Give me a chance. Let me be your Dom. I get what I want, you get what you want."

"I guess you've forgotten why I'm living with you..."

He closed his eyes like he was insulted, taking a deep breath before he opened them again. "Hank is a psychopath and a criminal. I don't assault, stalk, and rape women. Maybe it's hard to understand because you've never tried it, but it's completely different. It's beautiful, powerful...you'll enjoy it."

"I don't know, Calloway..."

"I can give you what you need. I can make love to you every night. I can take you out to dinner, hold you, whatever you want. And we can do what I want at different times. I think that's more than fair."

There was nothing I wanted more than to have

Calloway again. My blood screamed for him. "Calloway, there's nothing I want more...but I just can't handle it. Hank just assaulted me less than a week ago. I couldn't let you tie me up and punish me. I just can't handle that..."

"I wouldn't tie you up unless you asked me to. We never have to do anything you don't want to do. I don't think you understand, Rome."

"No, I do understand," I whispered. "You said a Dom/sub relationship is about trust, right?"

He nodded.

"I don't trust you—or anyone—enough to have that kind of relationship. It's nothing personal, Calloway."

"But it is personal," he whispered. "I would never hurt you."

"But you get off on hurting women. It doesn't make any sense."

"But the women enjoy the hurt—because it feels good—"

"No." The more we talked about it, the more convinced I was that I couldn't handle it. After being prey to so many different men in so many different circumstances, I couldn't do it anymore. I wanted a normal relationship where I felt equally powerful. I couldn't give Calloway all the control because I needed some of it to feel safe. There was no way around it. "I'm sorry…"

He bowed his head in disappointment. "It's okay… I understand."

I couldn't sit at the dinner table with him any longer. Looking at him hurt too much. I wanted to crawl into his lap and wrap my arms around his neck, feeling safe against his powerful body. But I couldn't do that. Instead, I left my dinner untouched, determined to eat it later, and left the kitchen—returning to the solitude of my room.

I felt perfectly safe in his house, knowing Hank wouldn't be able to get to me even if he knew I was there, but I still couldn't sleep. After sharing Calloway's bed last night, I knew I would never get a good night's rest across the hall from him. There was something about his body heat, his rhythmic breathing, and his smell that lulled me to sleep like a lullaby. After the difficult conversation we'd had earlier, I shouldn't get close to him.

But I was too weak.

I gently rapped my knuckles against the door as I opened it.

He lay on his back with his face pointed to the ceiling. The sheets were bunched around his waist, and his hand rested on his chest. "Come here." He pulled the sheets back so I could join him, just as wide awake as I was.

I slipped in between the covers and cuddled into his side, immediately feeling better once he was beside me. His powerful body was a natural heater, emitting warmth that absorbed into the cotton sheets.

He wrapped his strong arms around me and held me close, feeling like a dream. His lips brushed my hairline, and he sighed in contentment once I was beside him. "There's something I'd like to say."

"Okay…"

"The first time we met, you slapped me in that bar—three times."

"Yes…I remember." I was still embarrassed about it.

"I didn't tell you to stop because I liked it. I liked the pain, the crack of your palm against my cheek. I liked the way my skin lit on fire from the heat. I liked the rage in your eyes, the satisfaction you received from punishing me. My cock had never been harder, and all I wanted to do was bend you over the bar and fuck you."

My heart rate spiked from his honesty—as well as arousal.

"That's what I want us to have. That scorching, sexy

kind of pain that feels so good. It's not about hurting you to get off. It's about both of us experiencing the same adrenaline, the same rush. I want you to understand that."

I knew he really wanted to get his way, but no matter what he said, I was too stubborn to change my mind. I loved this man—still. And I had a feeling I would always love this man. But love wasn't enough to overcome my past, to allow someone to use me like I'd been used before. I'd been down that road too many times. No more.

Calloway knew his words had no effect on me. He sighed then buried his face into my neck. His comforting arms wrapped around me again, and he pulled my leg over his hip, exactly where he liked it. His cock pressed against me, long and thick. But he didn't try to have sex with me even though he probably could have seduced me if he'd tried.

I hated disappointing him.

But I didn't want to disappoint myself.

18

CALLOWAY

I escorted her to work, to lunch, and back home again—like clockwork. I wanted to know where she was at all times so that motherfucker couldn't make another pass at her. As the days went by and her bruises disappeared, calm slowly emerged.

But I would always be pissed underneath.

I tried getting Rome to reconsider my offer. I even offered her a compromise.

But she wouldn't take it.

In the beginning, I was attracted to her fire, her stubbornness. I loved her strength and her ability to command a room despite her small stature. But now, it was seriously biting me in the ass.

She was unwilling to accept anything less than what she deserved.

Despite my annoyance, I actually respected her for it.

And that just made me want her more.

It was a vicious cycle. I wanted this woman so badly, but I couldn't have her. Several times, I considered caving and just giving her what she wanted. Maybe I wouldn't be a Dom anymore, but at least I would still have her. I enjoyed spending time with her, sleeping with her, and everything else that came with the package.

But could I hide my dark side forever?

Probably not.

I sat in my office at Humanitarians United and looked out the window and across the city. Hank was out there somewhere, living his life like a cockroach under the sink. I would find him, and very soon, I would squash him with my shoe. He had no idea I was coming for him, that he'd pissed off a powerful man who shouldn't be provoked.

Rome would get her revenge. I'd see to it.

At the end of the day, I walked to her office and announced my presence silently, with just a look.

Even though her back was to me, she picked up on my arrival. She looked at me with those beautiful emeralds for eyes then packed up her things to leave.

She wore a tight skirt and a formfitting blouse. Her legs looked unbelievable in her skirt.

I wanted to fuck her so bad.

Six weeks had come and gone without sex. I was going crazy, and I wondered if she was going crazy too.

She had to be.

We left the building, ignoring everyone's prying looks as we passed. Everyone knew we were sleeping together, and that was just fine with me. Dean was skittish around me, realizing he'd hit on the boss's lady. He probably thought he was going to get fired at any moment.

Good.

We returned to the house, and like we were still a couple, she made dinner in the kitchen while I showered in my bedroom. I was tempted to beat off with my shampoo, but I stopped myself. Jerking off was never as much as fun as the real thing. I would much rather have been sliding my cock through her wet pussy than my hand.

I dried off and got dressed before I went downstairs, sexually frustrated like never before. Anger and rage welled inside me, not because I expected sex from Rome in exchange for letting her live with me, but because I just wanted her so much.

We ate dinner in silence. I didn't bother making

conversation because I was afraid I would command her to bend over the table and lift up her skirt. I'd had the fantasy before, especially when I was sitting at my desk in my office.

After dinner, we sat on the couch and watched TV. Rome worked on paperwork from her side of the couch, and I read a book even though I wasn't interested in it. My cock hardened on and off throughout the night, and the constant shift of my blood just put me in a worse mood.

Eventually, I just went to bed.

I needed space from her. I couldn't look at her legs without picturing them around my waist. I couldn't look at those lips and not picture them wrapped around my cock. I couldn't stop picturing my cock buried inside her asshole.

So I lay in bed, still hard and utterly frustrated.

An hour later, she gently knocked on the door and cracked it open.

Of course, I wanted to sleep with her. Something about her presence allowed me to drift away, nightmare-free. But right then, I wasn't in the mood for sleeping. Everything was catching up with me, my lack of control, my lack of sex, and my general rage.

This time, she didn't ask to come inside. She just walked in.

"If you get in this bed, I'm gonna kiss you. And then I'm gonna fuck you." I gave her a fair warning, wanting her to understand what kind of mood I was in. I wasn't interested in snuggling unless my cock was buried inside her at the same time. "So, I suggest you stay in your room tonight."

She stood still on the carpet, halfway between the bedroom and the bed. In the same t-shirt she always wore, she looked sexy in the shapeless fabric. Her hair stretched down her chest, and her beautiful legs could be seen underneath. She watched me with an indecipherable expression.

I waited for her to walk out, but I hoped she wouldn't go anywhere.

She grabbed her shirt and slowly pulled it over her head, revealing her perfect tits and the black thong underneath.

Oh god.

Her fingers trailed down her body, over her round tits and down her stomach, to the lace of her panties. She fingered them before she pulled them down her long legs, kicking them aside.

Fuck.

She sauntered to the bed, her hips shaking as she moved.

Please don't be a dream. Please don't be a dream.

She crawled on the bed and up my chest, her long hair trailing against my body as she moved. Her legs parted and planted on either side of my hips. She pressed her lap down, her wet pussy touching the hot skin of my cock.

Definitely not a dream.

She leaned over me and pressed her lips to mine, her mouth soft and seductive.

My hand immediately dug into her hair, and I deepened the kiss, turning it aggressive and almost violent. My cock ached from the lack of attention it had received, and it wanted to be buried inside her so deep.

I gripped one of her tits and squeezed, feeling the soft skin and the hard nipple under my fingertips. I loved foreplay because I brought her to the edge before we even began, but I was too anxious to draw it out.

I grabbed the base of my cock and pressed the head into her entrance, feeling the slickness that began long before she walked through that door. I pushed inside her and slid all the way through, feeling her tightness like greeting an old friend. "Oh, fuck…" I gripped her hips and forced her lap on top of me, giving her every single inch. I closed my eyes and enjoyed the sensation, missing this feeling more than anything else in the world.

Rome gripped both of my wrists as she slowly

moved up and down, sliding my cock in and out of her. She squeezed me tightly, her pussy hardly acclimating to my large size. She bounced up and down, her tits shaking slightly as she moved.

I dug my thumbs into her stomach and rocked my hips into her, giving her my length over and over. We moved so well together, sliding past one another with fluidness. This pussy was made for my cock. "Rome..."

She moved faster, dropping down my length repeatedly. Her breathing sped up, her moans increasing in volume the longer we moved together. Her tits shook with force, and in record time, she tightened around me as she climaxed.

Say my name.

Her head rolled back as she screamed. "Calloway..."

Fuck yes.

When she was finished, I rolled her onto her back and positioned myself on top of her. I wanted to dominate her, to fuck her like she was mine. I pulled her legs around my waist just the way I liked then slammed into her hard, forcing my headboard to dent the wall. I moved in and out quickly, moaning and grunting as I got lost in the sex.

Her hands moved to my biceps, holding on as she

ground her hips against me. "I miss your come inside me…"

Holy fuck.

I locked my eyes to hers as I fucked her hard, my entire body moving with the momentum. My cock was harder than it'd ever been before, and I was on the precipice of the most powerful orgasm I'd ever experienced. I was excited to fill her, to give her more of myself than I ever had.

Her ankles locked around my waist, and her nipples hardened underneath me, feeling my cock throb just before release. Her nails dug into me, scratching the skin as she dragged down my arm.

I shoved my entire length inside her, my head nearly hitting her cervix, and I released with a moan louder than ever before. "Fuck…" There was no greater feeling than this, claiming the woman I was violently obsessed with. It was a supernatural experience, a connection to this woman who meant the world to me. It was lustful in nature, but so much more at the same time.

I remained buried inside her as I caught my breath, my body coated in sweat. She stayed underneath me, her nipples softening. I ran my tongue across her sweaty skin, tasting the salt off her body. My lips trailed up her neck and to her lips, kissing her with affection. "Sweetheart…"

She ran her fingers through my damp hair, her chest pressed to mine. "Sexy."

I buried my face in her neck, our breathing in tune. "I missed you." I didn't realize how much I truly missed her until then—when I was connected with her. How could I give this up? How could I walk away from the loveliest woman in the world?

I didn't think I could.

———

"You doing okay, man?" Jackson followed me into the office, showing concern rather than his true asshole self.

"I've been better." I told him about everything that happened to Rome. He didn't make a single smartass comment because he knew I was in a dark place. The fact that anyone had laid a hand on her made me sick to my stomach.

"Can I do anything to help?"

"Actually, yes." I pulled out all the paperwork from the drawer. "I'm signing everything over to you. Ruin is yours." I dropped the paperwork on the desk and grabbed a pen. "Just sign here."

"Whoa...what?" He approached the desk and looked down, seeing the deed and ownership papers. "Are you out of your mind?"

"No." I fell into the chair, knowing it was the last time I would sit there. "At least, I hope not."

"What brought this on?"

After the sex we had a few hours ago, I knew what I had to do. I wasn't happy about it, but I couldn't live without that woman. If I had to make this sacrifice, I would. It was better than being miserable all the time. "I'm giving Rome what she wants. I have to walk away from Ruin. Otherwise, the temptation will be too much. I think you can handle it."

"Are you sure?"

"Yes." I pushed the papers toward him. "Good luck."

"Uh…" He ran his hand through his hair. "What if you just do the paperwork, and I run the place? That's not a big deal, right?"

"I can't be associated with this place anymore," I said calmly. "It'll just stimulate me in ways I can't handle." Seeing subs in chains, averting their gaze until their masters gave them permission, would just make me want to overpower Rome. I could feel it in my bones. "I wouldn't be giving this to you if I didn't think you could handle it. You can always call me if you need help."

He continued to stare at the paperwork, his hands

on his hips. "Maybe you should take some time to think about it."

"I've already had plenty of time to think about it. Just sign it." I opened the drawer and pulled out the small black box. When I opened the lid, I saw the black diamond ring that I wanted to give to Rome. She wouldn't be my submissive, but I wanted her to wear it anyway. It was the one compromise she could give me, that I would still possess her in my world even if I was no longer in it. I placed it in my pocket then pushed the pen closer to my brother. "Come on, man. I've got somewhere to be."

"So, you're going vanilla?" he asked. "Once and for all."

I hoped it would be forever. "Yes."

"And you want to give me Ruin?" He repeated the questions like I wasn't sure what I was agreeing to.

"Jackson, I'm not an idiot. Just sign the papers, and let's move on."

He finally grabbed the pen and added his name to the dotted line. He signed all the paperwork then returned it to the desk, his shoulders sagging slightly with his newfound responsibility. "I wish you the best of luck, man. I hope she's worth it."

I still couldn't believe she'd broken me. I'd never bent so far for any woman in my life. I'd always just put my offer on the table, and if they didn't take it, they could walk away. But Rome changed who I was, in both good and bad ways. I'd never met a woman so strong, so capable. She stole all my attention, made me want to part with my old ways just so I could keep her. If I felt this strongly about her, perhaps I needed to listen to the advice my mother gave me. "She is."

CPSIA information can be obtained
at www.ICGtesting.com
Printed in the USA
LVOW13s2127270617

539565LV00018B/497/P